Tyne O'Connell divides her time between LA and the Isle of Wight where she lives with her two husbands. Her previous books include *Sex, Lies and Litigation, Latest Accessory* and *What's A Girl To Do?*. She is currently working on a sitcom adaptation of *What's A Girl To Do?* for American television.

Praise for Tyne O'Connell:

'An entertaining romp' *Options*

'Lightning-fast comic twists' *Elle*, Australia

'[Tyne O'Connell] delivers some superbly sassy one-liners in this hilarious romp. Definitely a book for the modern girl' *Chat*

'Hilarious comedy of errors' *Good Book Guide*

'Well might this be called a girlie novel for the nineties' *Oxford Mail*

'Ex-pat Australian author O'Connell's debut is an extremely sure-footed romp, spiced with spot-on bad-taste humour, à la Kathy Lette and the *Ab Fab* team, and some excellent characterisation. Bravo!' *Who Weekly*

Check out the Tyne O'Connell website:
www.tyne-oconnell.demon.co.uk

GU00707494

Making the A-List

Tyne O'Connell

review

First published in 1999
by REVIEW

An imprint of Headline Book Publishing

10 9 8 7 6 5 4 3 2 1

ISBN 0 7472 7301 4

Typeset by Palimpsest Book Production Limited,
Polmont, Stirlingshire
Printed and bound in Great Britain by
Clays Ltd, St Ives plc

Headline Book Publishing
A division of Hodder Headline PLC
338 Euston Road
London NW1 3BH

For Martin and Albert

Acknowledgements

The gratitude goes on. Writing a book set in the London contemporary art world involved a lot of research and a strong liver. How lucky I am, then, to be married to an artist who could attend all the openings and drink all the Becks beer for me. Thanks therefore goes to Eric Hewitson and the art world at large for providing me with the inspiration, the setting and the vodka (beer makes me bloat).

As always I am grateful for the tough love of Rupert Wilkes and Martin Gibson who were *free* but not too *easy* with their advice and editing.

V. special thanks to The Girls; Vivienne Schuster at Curtis Brown and Geraldine Cooke, Mary-Anne Harrington and Imogen Aylen at Headline, not just for being so clever but for doing what they do with flair.

Most of all, huge hugs and kisses to my remarkable family, especially Zad, Kajj and Cordelia for not minding that I'm not a bit handy, can't cook, clean, open bills or work out how to use remote controls.

Things I Long to Experience before Turning Thirty

1   Be interviewed by *Vogue* about my opinions on British Art.
2   Make love in a hallway because I can't wait to get to the bedroom.
3   Fall in love at first sight.
4   Receive a proposal of marriage (I don't necessarily want to say yes).
5   Kiss all the way home in a taxi.
6   Lie about where I spent the night.
7   Join an exclusive health club such as Groucho's (all that witty repartee must be good for you).
8   Be a real size ten.
9   Have a bank balance written in black ink rather than red.
10 New York.

Being dropped is v. unpleasant. The great minds of the twenty-first century want to get their shit together on this one. Forget discovering the secret to immortality and world peace, they want to focus their grant money on finding a palliative for being dumped.

It doesn't matter what your IQ, your postcode or your income bracket, nothing can cushion the blow of being chucked.

Even for perfect size tens with brilliant career prospects who know that the next boyfriend is just around the corner, being dumped can annihilate a girl's self-image. For a size twelve with a thigh complex, though, bouncing back is even harder – especially when the big Three-0 is looming.

Some people will tell you that turning thirty is no different to turning twenty-nine, but we all know that's bollocks. A bit like when your parents tell you 'These are the best years of your life', when you're thirteen and covered in pimples.

I had Turning Thirty pencilled into my diary for three weeks' time – although I was still hoping to cancel if I got a better offer. Last month I had even requested another birth certificate in the hope of finding that I actually had another year up my sleeve. Forget it.

Thirty is a benchmark age like twenty-one and thirty-five and thirty-nine. You can tell yourself that it means nothing, that it's just a number, but then again, you can tell yourself that you'll fit into a size eight – doesn't mean you will. From age thirty I would have to stop referring to myself as a girl, wearing kitten heels with bare legs and buying my clothes on the Portobello Road.

Normally when my self-esteem has taken a thrashing, I'll go shopping. Not Bond Street or Knightsbridge – my pay packet doesn't extend that far, and besides, even though I might covet the window displays of Prada or Dolce & Gabbana, I'm actually a refusenik as far as fashion goes. My girlfriends call me a 'runway refugee'.

I faced this fact years ago as a teenager, actually. Even designer clothes come out like anarchic battle dress on me. It's genetic – my father was a mountain climber and my mother was, like most middle-class English mothers of her time, a Burberry bag lady.

I'm far happier in a mini boasting bare legs (hopefully without too many shaving cuts) and a knee-length leather coat. Or even better, a pair of jeans and tee shirt nicked from my latest lover. There is something v. rewarding about managing to slip into a slim-hipped ex-boyfriend's Calvin Kleins.

But this time, not even the promise of squeezing into my ex's jeans could lift me from the well of my misery. That's how bad it was. You see, this was no ordinary dropping; this was a dropping of my own making, a more or less auto-dropping, in that I had virtually hounded the love of my life into dumping me. Only I didn't realise that he was the love of my life until after he dumped me. Obviously. One never does.

In fact, I'd even flirted with the idea of dumping him a few days earlier. But now that I'd been dropped I was able to see that Emmanuel was actually my soulmate all along. My sense of loss was overwhelming.

Now, here I was, on the morning after this historic dumping, slumped over the triangular glass desk at A SPACE, the hipper-than-formaldehyde gallery off Bond Street. No doubt you've heard of it – it was at the vanguard of all those late nineties Cool Britannia artists that pickled their bodies, etc., etc. V. old hat now, of course, v. file-your-nails-and-yawn stuff. Still, it was art.

Out of the corner of one eye, I watched potential buyers walk past, look in, spot me dribbling over my desk and then scuttle off. I had to face it. I was scaring customers away.

Brilliant, my better self taunted my deeply self-pitying self; just when you are totally dependent on commission, you start frightening off the punters.

I laid my head on the cool surface of the desk and watched my breath mist up the glass. I might even have said something pathetic that girls stopped saying, like, a century ago, such as 'God, I'm pointless'. Basically I was in a seriously regressive state. If someone had started singing a Chris De Burgh song at that moment, I probably would have joined in.

It had all started with a list, which sounds harmless in itself but, as any solicitor will tell you, putting things in writing can land you in court or worse. This was worse. I've never had any problems over my lists before. I've always made lists. Gertrude Whitney Vanderbilt always made lists too. I'm a List girl rather than an It girl.

The problem with this list, though, was that I showed it to my boyfriend Emmanuel. Ironically the list was meant to help him understand me. Only I wasn't laughing.

It was my therapist's idea to show it to him, natch.

God, how had I been so stupid? I mean, who actually takes their therapist's advice? What kind of schmuck was I? Just thinking about Emmanuel's reaction when he'd read the list made me want to tear my hair out in fistfuls.

I think the point where I requested a blanket ban on all sport hit him the hardest. His face had practically slid off his head like he'd been scalped or something.

After that he'd gone berserk. He'd expressed himself more eloquently in English than he'd ever managed before. When he'd exhausted his Berlitz vocab, he'd run out v. passionately. It was my impression at the time that he wasn't planning to return. There were no au revoirs.

He was probably the one true love of my life, I realised now as I draped myself pathetically across on my desk, and I had driven him away with my petty needs. That was another list I was working on, a list in progress so to speak: a list of desires unsuitable in a thirty-year-old girl/woman.

My desires too were becoming a bit of a problem these days. When I was in my early twenties I didn't have a need to rub together. Back then my life was a series of wants and whims, but recently I had felt overwhelmed by longings that seemed to lunge out of me in the most awkward situations. Sometimes I would be making love or snuggling up against a lover's back and wham, there they were – my needs and longings. Destroying near perfect bliss.

I had hoped that writing those longings down might bring me closer to fulfilling them, but the list just seemed to grow longer and longer and less and less achievable.

People who write things down are more likely to be successful. They did a survey at Yale and discovered that only six per cent of graduates had a clear idea of what their goals were, and out of that six per cent, it was the one per cent who wrote those goals down who achieved what they longed for.

I write a lot of lists. Gertrude Whitney Vanderbilt (my idol) who started the Whitney Museum was a big list-maker too. In fact, practically everything that is known about her was gleaned from the lists she made.

My lists range from lists of items I need to add to my wardrobe, to things I really must do, like start a pension plan. I even keep a hit list. That was another list that Emmanuel took umbrage at. But, like I told him, every sophisticated girl has a hit list; it's part of the new immorality sweeping the world. Lots of girls must wonder what the world would be like if, say, their boss wasn't in it.

It doesn't mean you're not a nice person just because you'd like to see someone who makes you feel dreadful taken out of the frame, does it? Let's face it, if they started offering contract killers over the counter, London would be a bloodbath by lunchtime.

Most of my family, my boss, several old boyfriends and all my fellow commuters on the Central line have made it onto my hit list at one time or another. I've even ended up there myself on occasion, when I've done something so stupid that I shouldn't be allowed to go on living.

My most pointless list, though, was the list I started five years ago based on what I wanted to achieve by age thirty. With the mad confidence of a girl still in her mid-twenties, I had hoped to be the proud owner of my own gallery, in a fulfilling relationship (or two) and a size ten.

Obviously it wasn't looking v. likely now. On top of my shit career prospects and size twelve dress size, I'd been chucked. Talk about grim. Now was the time to start gathering boyfriends, laying them down for the future, so to speak. It certainly wasn't the time for driving them away.

Let's face it, my chances of getting another boyfriend at this late stage were next to dismal. All the good-looking men with sound hygiene codes were either gay or taken. Hoping to find Mr Right after thirty was a bit like turning up to the January sales in February: chances were I was going to walk away with the male equivalent of lime-green hot pants with tassels. I was going to have to take what I could get.

Looking at my reflection in the glass of the desk, I saw an emotionally disfigured girl. I was scarred by my lover's rejection. I needed emotional surgery and even then, those in the know would probably be able to spot the scalpel marks.

I looked down at my bare legs, a bit cut up after a shave with a blunt Gillette. They were sticking out from my latest

Portobello find, a brown leather seventies mini, and I began to wonder if it was actually my legs that had turned him off me. I mean, maybe it wasn't the list after all, I reasoned, trying to back out of the blame.

It seems so unfair that a girl's own body can work against her aim to be a total head-turning babe that every man desires and every woman envies, but there it was. My body was on a counter-mission to expose me as size twelve instead of the size eight I longed to be.

My body was a bitch who took every opportunity to make me look less than perfect. My upper legs being the main offender, they were unbelievably disloyal: even after I'd started buying those fifteen-denier tights that make your legs look incredibly thin, they had managed to bulge.

Just then my boss walked in and gave me the afternoon off to 'sort myself out'.

Hello? Was I dreaming? I looked at him curiously for signs of mania. If you knew my boss, you'd realise how deeply troubling this was. I mean, normally I had to lose an eye to get a ten-minute lunch break, let alone a whole afternoon off.

I know that people outside the art world think of it as an easy ride, say, compared to accountancy and law but the truth is, art is peopled by cut-throat businessmen and cut-your-heart-out artists. But despite my boss's uncharacteristic largesse, this was not the kind of mess that was going to be sorted out in an afternoon, and I told him as much.

'Don't you realise,' I'd said to him, 'that my life is *over*?'

He'd looked at me briefly, in a sort of sneering way, before shaking his head and walking off. As far as my boss is concerned, my life never really got off the ground in the first place.

Still, not one to look gift horses in the mouth, I seized the moment and rang Sophie, my best friend of ten years, to see if she wanted to come out and play. Her assistant told me that she was 'unavailable'. This deflated me even further; the word 'available' held an extra poignancy for me today, feeling, as I did, v. much *available*.

I could never seem to reach Sophie these days; we'd hardly seen each other in weeks, which was a big change given our years of history together. She was a genuine fashion cognoscente with a black belt in looking good. Like I said, I was a runway refugee with more sass than class, so between us I guess we were a complete woman.

Sophie was no doubt extremely busy being a hotshot editor on *Class* magazine. I imagined her flying around in taxis, chatting on her mobile phone, heading for editorial meetings on the fifth-floor restaurant of Harvey Nichols.

Sophie was a girl with a real career, unlike my dogsbody job. She was a girl men fell over themselves to worship. When she eased on a pair of fifteen denier tights, her thighs did what they were supposed to do. Which meant that even if I had got on to her, there was probably no way she'd understand my plight. She had no reference point for this kind of angst. God, I was feeling sorry for myself.

Next I rang my flatmate Alice and pleaded with her to dig me out of my depression. Alice was much more understanding. She was American and positive and impossibly enthusiastic in a cool 'whatever' kind of New York way. She's been in therapy all her life, and has answers where I only have lists of questions.

Being the brick she is, she agreed to get the afternoon off and meet me in a bar off Hoxton Square near the gallery where she works. She hinted at vodka drinking, and I saw her point immediately.

My List of lists

1   The list of all the men I had wanted to sleep with before I turned thirty. An amended version of the list of all the men I had wanted to sleep with before I turned twenty.
2   The list of friends, family and co-workers I am never going to speak to again because they are eroding my self-esteem.
3   The list of foods I am never going to allow to pass my lips again – anything solid and pleasant-tasting, basically. Anyone who doesn't know me might think I have an eating disorder.
4   The list of foods I am determined to gorge on at every opportunity, for instance, anything that tastes nasty and has no calories, especially wheatgrass, alfalfa, royal jelly syrup, etc.
5   Hit list. List of all people I would like to hire a trained marksman to deal with.

Slipping my feet back into my one-size-too-small, vintage black satin shoes, a find in a jumble sale in my old home town of Horsham, I set off. Hiding behind my Gucci sunglasses (still paying for them on my Visa) and grabbing my Prada holdall (circa 1995), I dragged myself down to Bond Street tube. Head down, shoulders slumped, I was in my don't-even-think-about-trying-to-sell-me-a-sprig-of-heather pose.

I was interrogating my inner self with a series of questions to which there would never be answers. I had some serious self-emasculating to do.

1   What was I thinking of, writing a list of what I need from a relationship?
2   Was I insane?
3   Was I suffering from lead poisoning, ie: had I been breathing too heavily around Oxford Circus again?
4   Where was my brain? My mother was always asking that question.

'Where is your brain, girl?' she'd ask whenever I did perfectly normal stuff like buy a dress that was obviously a size too small. You can't be too fussy with second-hand clothes. They either fit or you force yourself into them.

This dumping, though, was my worst nightmare. To be back on the shelf before my thirtieth birthday! Maybe it

, me who needed to be taken out of the frame. Perhaps I should pop into a pharmacist and ask how many paracetamol I would have to take to bring to a definitive end this hell that my life had become.

I mean, I didn't want to make as big a mess of my suicide as I had of my life and end up wiping out all my major organs. Doomed to spend my life strung up to a drip and a monitor, exhibited on *News at Six* and discussed in Parliament.

As I elbowed my way through the lunchtime shoppers on Oxford Street, it came to me that if only I'd been born dyslexic, and didn't know how to write stuff down, none of this would have happened. Actually, come to think of it, there was a fear once that I might be dyslexic.

In the first year of school, I'd had such a lot of trouble getting my letters the right way round and spelling and so on, that eventually my mother had made a fuss (as was her wont).

A specialist came to the school, a nice woman with long brown hair and a lovely smile. She gave me this test and told me that if I did really well I would get a chocolate frog, and of course I did beautifully and it turned out that I wasn't dyslexic at all, just bone lazy. Far from getting a chocolate frog or something nice like that, I was given a smack by my mother and extra homework by my teacher.

But now it occurred to me that maybe the test marker had got it wrong. Or maybe I was having a sort of relapse that day. Yes, that seemed likely, I'm always having relapses – especially on my diets. Maybe I was reverting?

I started to feel a bit better, virtually convinced that someone else had written the incriminating list, until a smarty-pants voice in my head taunted, 'You're grasping at straws, girl. You've been writing without a hitch for years. You got an A in English. Face it, Saskia,' I muttered while I searched through the madness of my bag for my weekly tube pass.

I often talk to myself when I'm looking for something in my bag on the street because it gives potential attackers the impression that I'm madder than I am. Even violent criminals prefer a saner quality of prey when they can get it.

Anyway, this whole fiasco was my therapist's fault. He was the one who had made me show the list to Emmanuel. At the bottom of every mess there's a man smiling smugly, and this mess was no different.

My therapist, Albert of St James, was the real demon in this disaster. Didn't the man see how all this would end? He'd always encouraged me in my list-making – now I was drowning in them. My room was strewn with them.

When she'd first moved in, Alice had warned me that if I ever did commit suicide, or die accidentally, there would be a massive investigation. She said that years of police time would be wasted as the homicide squad searched for significance in my lists.

Which got me thinking.

Some of those lists were indeed extremely incriminating. The police wouldn't know what had hit them once they started deciphering them. With what would they begin the investigation? My hit list, maybe?

That could be v. nasty, exposing as it did a particularly ugly side of my normally lovely nature. Bit embarrassing really, but now that we have entered the era of the new immorality it was practically a self-growth step. A self-awareness exercise, yes, that's what it was – an exploration of my psyche. Just the same, a list like that could probably give the police ideas.

As I pushed my fellow commuters further into the death trap of the carriage so that I could squeeze on, I started to think about suing Albert.

A frazzled-looking tourist said, 'Well! Really!' and looked at me with a please-don't-mug-me-or-bash-me-and-leave-me-bleeding-at-the-side-of-the-track expression as I sat on her lap. I don't like using the laps of innocent tourists normally, but it had to be done. I simply had to sit somewhere – my shoes were killing me! Absolutely squeezing the life out of me, they were. I tried to explain this but she didn't speak English, and the more I pointed at my shoes, the more she thought I was going to kick her.

I smiled at my shocked tourist in a welcome-to-Cool-Britannia tourist-board kind of way, and made myself cosy on her big comfy lap.

What kind of therapist was Albert, asking me to expose my inner longings to a man like Emmanuel? It was probably something he'd read in *Therapists Are Us* magazine.

Whatever the antecedents, he had me eating out of the palm of his hand by the end of a session. He'd look at me over those long lashes of his, flick his shiny black hair into its sexier-than-thou fascist parting and grin mischievously, the way he always does when he's about to say something really wicked and evil and side-splittingly funny.

I was hypnotised by Albert's belief that Emmanuel would want to know what it was I really wanted from the relationship. Albert could be v. convincing actually. I was high on post-coitus pheromones at the time of handing the said list over.

Albert had been most specific about the timing of the handing-over. He'd made it sound trickier than a weapons decommissioning. Yes, he had been most insistent, and v. sloshed now I think of it. After telling me to give Emmanuel the list, he'd opened a second bottle of champagne and got carried away in the moment, blow-drying my hair into a crazy bouffant that was still noticeable today.

Well, all right, I may as well come clean. Albert's not a real therapist. Not in the went to college and got a licence to hand out advice sort of way, anyway. Albert's more your chat-as-you-cut-and-blow-dry style of therapist.

OK, so he's my hairstylist, but you know the thing – taste to die for, brilliant at giving advice about relationships that he never takes himself and hold-your-legs-together gorgeous. (Gay, of course.) Just the sort of bloke a girl in distress likes to turn to.

In my experience, hairstylists are so much more useful than bona fide therapists, and anyway, even if the advice is shit, you still get a nice blow-dry at the end of it. Although after this list fiasco I may be forced to review my source of counselling from here on in. I made a mental note to add Albert's name to my hit list, which soothed me slightly.

There was no doubt that this What I Want from a Relationship list had ruined my life. Tomorrow I would ring a solicitor and set the wheels of litigation in motion. Yes, that was the spirit. Surely destroying my last chance at having a significant other must be worth something in a court of law in the free world.

Was England the free world, though? I mulled this over as the train rattled onward through subterranean London. My fellow commuters and I looked at the floor and tried to ignore the stream of beggars, buskers and roaming insane people that paraded through our carriage asking for handouts, applause and, in the case of one violently mad bloke with a trolley, our teeth.

I was still considering this free-world issue as a suit, strap-hanging above me, knocked my tourist in the face with his briefcase. She let out a sort of deflated whimpering sound; my heart went out to her.

I looked at her with my tourist-board smile of reassurance but I could tell she was having a tough time of it, what with me on her lap and the bald guy with the briefcase knocking her head about. She wasn't having an easy ride in Cool Britannia.

So when the briefcase Nazi did it again, I decided to be a Good Samaritan by planting a well-aimed elbow in his groin. He reacted the way women always do when men feel their bum on a train and moved quietly but purposefully down the carriage. That was more like it. My tourist babbled gratefully – at least, I hope it was gratefully, she was a bit distressed all in all.

At Bank, I thanked my tourist for the use of her lap, gave the briefcase Nazi a warning look and changed onto the Northern line.

Needy! That's what Emmanuel had said I was. He couldn't have hurt me more if he'd slapped me across the face. Needy? Me? I ask you, was requiring the right side of the bed and half the duvet needy?

OK, so I also admitted to wanting to be put on a pedestal, and something trivial about not always wanting to pay half every time we went for a drink, and appreciating the odd gift, breakfast in bed and a poem or something when he could manage it.

Big deal. I like a bit of romance in my life, so sue me. Was he *sooooo* shocked to hear that stuff? I'm sure I've mentioned it all in passing along the way, anyway; I mean, I'm not a total cellulite-gazer, I do have a brain and the guts to put my case every now and then.

Maybe the list was going the wrong way about it, though.

I thought he'd say something about accepting the list overall, but that he had a problem with the sport ban. Which would have given me the chance to be all United Nations about it and agree to let him read the results of the World Cup final, say, in return for access to all his previous history with girls and the right to demand monogamy. After that he'd see how giving I could be, and we would have the most brilliant sex ever and agree that our love was on a higher plane. But to call me needy! To say I was trying to pin him down, to distort his fine Gallic character! It was too much.

He said he'd never seen anything so ridiculous as the list in his life, which I find a bit unlikely, given his career as an art critic. The cruellest cut was that *he* had been the one to walk out. If a relationship has to end – and let's get real, they usually do, just look at the stats – I want it to be ended by me. Usually I manage to cotton on to the fact that a relationship has run its course and nip in with the closure.

I've made a list of clues that a guy wants out. Things like breaking a few dates in a row, sleeping with my best friends, etc., give off the warning signals that allow me to step in and cut the cord, as if it was my idea. As if I had better things to do with my life than date a low-down heel like him. As if.

I know I'm going to sound really precious, but I'm *always* the one who does the dumping if there's any dumping to be done. And it's not just me, either; statistically it is usually the girl who breaks it off. It's part of the new immorality drive that we girls are on, part of taking control of our destiny, only not in an overbearing I've-got-testicles-too kind of way.

The new immorality is all about knowing yourself and caring deeply about getting your way. Whereas once I would have bought tawny-brown moisturising foundation because the girl at the counter convinced me that an orange, streaky face suited me, now I'll have the strength of my own opinion to say 'Forget it.' More or less.

The new immorality is all about living the kind of life that *Cosmopolitan* says you can. A life of getting the coolest score in all the quizzes like, *Do you know your desires as well as you know your cellulite?* And *Be in touch with your personal bliss!*

The new immorality is saying yes to success and no to failure. Yes to eating, no to cooking. Yes to designer interiors, no to doing your own cleaning. It's all about shrugging your shoulders at what other people think of you.

All about having that 'whatever' chic that girls with really long legs and careers with publicity agents enjoy. Living for the moment, being in touch with your bliss. However there is a bit of a catch actually, a tricky bit I've yet to master: part of the new immorality is not making your happiness dependent on the feelings or behaviour of another person.

Only now was I beginning to have doubts about this new immorality. Maybe the kick to the groin would have been more effective with Emmanuel. Maybe, just as Emmanuel was leaving, instead of shrugging my shoulders and pretending not to give a stuff, I should have yelled, 'No, you don't! If there is any dropping to be done here, I'm the girl to do it!'

Besides, men are meant to go on loving all the women they have ever loved; it's all part of Lad Culture. Men are meant to be gutted when a relationship ends, and would happily have no-strings sex with all their old lovers again if the opportunity came up and they could get away with it.

That's why I was so peeved. Emmanuel had said nothing of no-strings sex later on down the track. In fact, he'd been rather sneering about our future sexual prospects together.

The first time a boyfriend dropped me, I'd cried for days and then told all my friends that I'd dropped him. I remember how impressed they'd all been that I could ditch someone so incredibly cute as Andy Bowen-Brown.

When Andy started the vicious rumour that he'd dropped me, I'd just snorted and said, 'What an ego!' Which seemed to satisfy my friends, who'd then joined me in a delicious lampooning session which lasted for days until one of them started dating Andy.

On this occasion it was clear who had dropped whom. Not that Emmanuel had actually said the words 'You're dropped', but by the way he'd looked at me after he'd crumpled up the list and thrown it at me, I more or less sensed that whatever there had been between Emmanuel and me was no more. Besides, he was too sophisticated and French, to state the obvious, thank God. At least I'd been saved that indignity.

I came out of Old Street station into bright sunlight, which was starting to break through the clouds that had been hanging over London like a grey umbrella all spring.

Once I got my bearings, I headed north-east towards Hoxton Square where I was to meet Alice.

My feet had started to swell a bit and my vintage shoes were hugging my feet so tightly I was worried the stitching would split. No doubt they were feeling a bit out of place and nervous about the area. Even though Alexander McQueen started out here, this part of London wasn't really vintage-satin-shoe territory. This was more your jackboot kind of postcode. I turned my bag around so that the Prada label wasn't showing, took off my sunglasses so that I could negotiate the broken pavements, the sewage leaks, the overflowing litter bins and the dog turds.

As I walked down Great Eastern Street, a bloke on a bicycle ran into me and would have knocked me down if I hadn't held onto an elderly pensioner in a woolly hat and a Zimmer frame for support. As he rode off, he swore at me and called me a name I'd never heard before.

The lady in the woolly hat told me to ignore him and shouted out 'Cheeky bastard!' I was still gripping her Zimmer.

'They're a bunch of little arseholes around here, love,' she told me, patting my hand kindly. 'You don't want to mind them. I always carry my stick with me and whack them on the back as they go past.'

I gave her a sisterly smile to show her that I was in tune with the new immorality, and walked on.

According to my girlfriend Alice, the only thing Emmanuel and I ever had together was a mutual love of Emmanuel. 'You're in love with the accent, not the man,' she'd always assured me.

But, like I told her, a little bit of French goes a lot further than a lot of Birmingham, which was where my last boyfriend came from. Thin chest, weedy legs, conceptual artist, drank his beer from the bottle, chain-smoked roll-ups and panted during sex. Make no mistake, *I* dropped *him*.

I know it's a cliché but I loved those filthy French nothings Emmanuel used to whisper in my ear while making wild Gallic love to me – which was most of the time we were together when you add it up. And that was another thing Albert had advised me to do.

'Add up the time you spend with Emmanuel and subtract the amount of time you were in the throes of lovemaking.'

Out of three months, I was left with forty-five minutes, and at least twenty minutes of that was spent watching him on the phone to his mother in Lyon – my phone. He still owed me for that call. And now he was gone, our relationship was over and I was back on the shelf. Well, more the bar, actually. Drowning my sorrows, I think it's called.

The Maybe list

1   Maybe if I'd arched my back more when we were making love.
2   Never shown him my upper thighs.
3   Always worn a Wonderbra.
4   Never spoken with my mouth full.
5   Never rung him.
6   Asked him more about his interests.
7   Faked more orgasms.
8   Asked for more sex/not demanded so much sex.
9   Never taken my make-up off at night.
10 Etc., etc., ad infinitum. Maybe he would still love me.

This list is usually followed by the From Now On list, and afterwards by embarrassing behaviour. All part of the healing process.

Alice worked in a fabulous up-and-coming Shoreditch gallery, the sort you read about in the papers where art shocks rather than goes with your curtains and sofa. Alice has that certain something that drives women and men wild. A size eight figure, complete with hand-span waist and pert breasts. But I loved her as if she was a size twelve anyway.

She told me that if I really was back on the shelf, I needed to be propped up so that other blokes could get a better look at me. 'And the best place to prop a girl up is at the bar,' she said.

It was a warm afternoon and Alice was wearing nothing other than her black lace bra and a pair of tight brown Alien Workshop trousers that strained around her slimmer-than-slim hips. She took her rollerblades off and dropped them on a table like a mujahedin might dump his weapons. If this were Bond Street, where I worked, everyone would have been staring, but here no one gave a shit. People came in half-dressed, overdressed, on bikes, with dogs, kids, sculptures attached to drips, smelling of turpentine, sweat and formaldehyde. Whatever.

I looked across at the sea of artists, gallery owners and the trendy and not-so-trendy Fulham dwellers trying unsuccessfully to pretend they belonged here amid the studied cool of the local loft-owning artistic community.

I recognised a lot of the Saatchi crowd, standing outside

with kids as art statements on their shoulders. Unfortunately I also spotted a guy who'd brought in his portfolio at our gallery last week. I was dreading being recognised by him and asked how Stuart had liked his work, so I dragged Alice over to a table in a dark corner where I could monopolise her properly.

'Do you think I'm needy?' I asked her after we'd ordered our first round. 'Honestly, now?'

Alice may look like a blonde bimbo with her perfect nose and Cupid's bow mouth, but she's far from stupid: she could see she was in a minefield. The words 'honestly now' were a big clue.

'In what sense?' she asked, hoping no doubt that I'd forget the question.

'What do you mean, in what sense? It's a yes or no question, Alice! No being the preferable answer. Now tell me the truth.' I glared.

'Well, no, then. Well, er, well, it depends. Sometimes.'

I put a bit more menace into my glare. 'When exactly? I've never been needy. Give me times and places.'

Alice burst out laughing, and after struggling to maintain my glare for a bit, so did I. I knew I was taking the whole thing too seriously, but as Alice would put it, it was 'something I needed to work through'.

'Everyone's needy sometimes, Sass, you wouldn't be human.'

I nodded miserably. She gave me a cuddle and her tenderness made the tears well up behind my eyes.

Alice patted my back like she was hoping for a burp or something. 'Emmanuel's a jerk. He wanted everything and was prepared to give nothing. So when you asked for something, he chucked you. He was a bastard, Sass, an utter bastard. You're well rid of him.'

'Hang on a minute, he didn't exactly *chuck* me,' I corrected, sitting up straight, wanting to knock that rumour down before it ruined what was left of my reputation in this town. 'He just walked out without saying "see you later", that's all. I just sense that the relationship may have run its course and Emmanuel feels the same way. It was a chucking by mutual consent, in which both parties agreed simultaneously to chuck the other.'

'Whatever,' she said, looking unconvinced. 'Fact remains, he was a real shit and you're better off without him.'

She was right, and I smiled to show I appreciated her wisdom, but I knew and she knew, as every girl who has ever broken up with a real *shit* knows, the he-was-a-real-shit-and-I'm-better-off-without-him theory takes a long time to sink in.

First comes the self-flagellation. The poor me's; the remembering how he was everything to me and, now I come to think of it, I loved the way he left his used condoms on the floor for me to slip on. Suddenly it struck me as cute the way he slept with his mouth open and wore his boxers for two days on the trot.

After the he-was-everything blues comes the Maybe list, which as every girl knows, is far more painful than the worst hangover you've ever had.

I pulled the list from my bag and read it out to Alice.

'Maybe if I'd kept my make-up on at night.

'Maybe if I'd never shown him my bare bum/cellulite/ thighs, etc.

'Maybe if I'd faked more orgasms/had louder, more expressive orgasms.

'Maybe if I hadn't eaten so much when we went out for dinner. Maybe if I hadn't eaten at all?

'Maybe if I hadn't admitted liking dumb, feel-good films so much.

'Maybe if I'd always worn a Wonderbra.

'Maybe if I'd worn more make-up/less make-up/no make-up?

'Maybe then, if I'd done all of the above and more,
   maybe then he would have kept loving me?
What do you think?'

She didn't respond. She'd sat impatiently through the
entire Maybe list, shaking her head and waving her arms
around at passing staff so she could order more alcohol,
doubles this time.

Alice had heard the Maybe list before, and she knew that
it was closely followed by the From Now On list, followed
by my list of vows to give up all manner of life-enhancing
activities such as eating and sleeping, etc.

'That's it, I'll never eat again!' I cried out dramatically to
the bar at large as I sank into my chair looking very much
as if my vertebrae had dissolved.

Alice rolled her eyes.

'I mean it!' I told her with the crazed look of a wasted
clubber telling you about their E trip. 'You will never see
food pass these lips again. In fact, alert the tabloids and the
television news teams after day three so they can monitor
my death like an installation. The Tate can show it during
my retrospective.'

'But you're not an artist,' she reminded me.

'No, but my death will be v. artistic, and I want it to sort
of act as a tribute to my, er . . .'

'Your what?'

'My love of Emmanuel.'

'Oh, pah-lease. That shit?'

'Maybe then Emmanuel will see what he has lost. Actually,
better get the camera crew in on day six. I should have lost at
least ten pounds by then – he's never seen me as a size eight.
That will shock him.'

Alice looked at me sceptically, basically because I was still
gobbling my way through our second bowl of bar snacks as
I spoke; the crumbs were going everywhere. I looked down

at my chest, which was covered in a mixture of olive stones and crisps, and realised that I was losing it.

Alice tried unsuccessfully to steer me onto saner territory, but I remained oblivious to logic. Meanwhile the bar continued to fill up, and the two spare chairs at our table were commandeered by a pair of nerdy girls who looked like they were on a day trip from the commuter belt of Surrey, Sussex or somewhere else deeply uncool.

We huddled into the shadows of our corner in case they got drunk and flirty and wanted to chat.

We ordered more drinks from an Australian waitress who had the sort of perfect body I really wasn't up to dealing with at that time. She had breasts where the rest of us had plans for silicone implants, and it reminded me of the time Emmanuel had lamented my lack of mammary and suggested I take out a loan in order to afford said implants.

Going over the items on my What I Want from a Relationship list with Alice for something like the millionth time, I asked her what was so bad about it anyway. Alice, like the good friend she is, agreed that the list was pure and good and that the problem lay with Emmanuel. But that didn't help either.

'How could he drop me, Alice? Tell me that much. I mean, be honest, would you drop a girl like me? Presuming you were a man, that is?'

Alice squeezed my hand and said, 'Of course not. Drink up.'

'I mean, I even made him coffee yesterday,' I explained on the verge of tears, remembering the exquisite selflessness of the act.

Alice reacted to my announcement like I'd just declared a propensity for fondue. 'You made the coffee?' she spluttered. 'That's got to be a first. What was it, instant?'

'Well maybe I didn't actually *make* it,' I said, looking sheepishly at my drink. 'But I nipped out to that coffee

bar place across the road in my bathrobe. Only by the time
he woke up, I'd drunk it myself.'

Alice rolled her eyes.

'He didn't get up till two! I went out in bare feet,' I
explained. 'I could have stepped on some glass or worse!
I've never done that for any man,' I told her, sniffing.

'Get a grip,' she scolded, lighting up a big fat cigar with her
butane lighter. The blue flame shot up, practically singeing
a fringe into my hair in the process. 'Besides, we're going to
New York soon, so you've got that to focus on.'

'Oh yeah, New York,' I muttered, turning away so she
wouldn't see my guilty expression.

'You *have* spoken to Stuart about taking time off to go to
New York with me, haven't you?'

'Of course I've *spoken* to him. I'm just not sure that he heard
the bit where I mentioned New York. His mind is on a lot of
other things, I explained.'

'God, you're a walkover, Saskia Williams. You know
you're entitled to holidays. When did you last have a break?'

'I'm having one now, aren't I?' I asked haughtily.

'You've never had one, have you?'

'Not this past eighteen months, no. I mean, I would have,
but then Jon left and, well, Stuart's not been the same. I can
hardly leave him in the lurch like that, can I? He more or
less depends on me.'

'He's a man,' she said simply. 'A grown man, and you are
not his mother. I'm sure he can manage without you for a
fortnight,' she insisted, staring at the butane flame as it licked
the end of her stogy into an ember.

'Yes, well, a knock's one thing but Stuart's life was torn
apart by what Jon did to him,' I explained.

'Give it a rest, Saskia. They ran a business together. The
business relationship went sour and Jon left. It happens
every day. It doesn't mean you have to throw yourself on
the funeral pyre of Stuart's self-pity. You've got a life too!'

'A life?' I shrieked. 'A life that's no longer worth living,' I reminded her. 'I'll be thirty soon.'

'So?'

'It's all right for you, you're only twenty-four. You've got years to get your career together and your boyfriends stacked up. My life is over. Emmanuel was my last chance at love. I'm a disfigured woman who's been dumped.'

'You said you weren't dumped, you said it was chucking by consensus,' she reminded me.

'Oh, don't be so bloody American,' I snapped before letting out another painful sob.

Alice blew a fog of smoke from her Cohiba into her empty glass and watched it curl out like steam from a cauldron. 'You were only with him two months,' she pointed out.

'Three,' I corrected.

'Whatever. You never went anywhere. You never did anything. You never talked to one another. God, Sass, you didn't even speak the same language.'

'I know,' I sobbed. 'But I loved him.'

'Loved him? Saskia, you never stopped complaining about him. You went on and on to anyone who'd listen about how you couldn't wait to get rid of him. You were just waiting for the right moment, you said.

'You even slept with that Dutch artist guy last month because you said your relationship with Emmanuel had run its course. You said he was selfish, boring, predictable and unreliable,' she reminded me, looking in the air as she counted off his sins on her fingers.

'Well, he's a man, you said so yourself. That doesn't mean I wasn't smitten. Besides, he was a great lover.'

She snorted.

'What?'

'You said he was "a sympathy fuck". And I quote, Tuesday last week before going out, "I s'pose I'll have to have sex with

him". And when I asked why you bothered, you said it was
because you felt sorry for him.'

'I'd just been with Albert. I was feeling all girly and silly.
I didn't mean it. Emmanuel was a fantastic lover, the best
sex I've ever had.'

Alice looked at me, shook her head despairingly and went
back to filling up her glass with smoke.

'What?' I pressed, sensing that my grief wasn't being taken
seriously.

'You also said you were waiting for the right moment to
dump him. You said he took you for granted and didn't
take you out anywhere. Face it, Saskia, Emmanuel was a
substitute boyfriend, the guy you dated because you couldn't
bear to face the fact that you're in love with Jon Tashco.'

I felt like I'd been slapped across the face when she
said those words. Jon had been Stuart's partner at the
gallery until about six months ago. And one of my closest
friends. After months of sniping, they had a huge fight about
something and split.

Jon had left the business to Stuart, but he'd taken all of
A SPACE's best artists, which, even as a believer in the new
immorality, I thought was v. low. That's why I'd stayed with
Stuart and turned down Jon's offer to join him at Tashco,
but more of that later. I hardly saw Jon any more. But the
real issue here was Alice's accusation that I carried a candle
to Jon.

'Absolutely untrue,' I told her. 'I mean, I think I'd be the
first to know if I fancied someone,' I snorted derisively.

Alice's baby-blue eyes rolled around their sockets in dis-
belief. She didn't have a lot of faith in my ability to judge
my own feelings. I'd known Alice for three months but as
far as she was concerned, she knew me better than I knew
myself. In fact, I'd met Alice after she went to work for Jon
as his assistant at his new gallery.

Sure Jon and I had flirted a bit, sure he had the greatest

face I'd ever seen off a jeans advert, the best sense of humour and a body I would have doubled my period cramps to see naked. But *fancy* him? Give me a break, he was ten years older than me. Technically he was old enough to be my father. Only the other day I read about a nine-year-old boy siring a healthy ten-pound baby girl. *Hello!* magazine, I think it was.

'Why do you say that I fancy Jon, anyway?' I demanded hotly.

Alice lifted her head from the smoke-filled glass and looked at me like my friend Sophie had looked at the girl at Harvey Nichols the other day, when she told her that grey was the new black.

'Pah-lease.'

'Pah-lease what?' I asked.

'Obvious, isn't it?'

'What do you mean *obvious*?' I asked.

She was holding the cigar between her teeth in the manner of a gangster. 'And he likes you, I can tell,' she assured me.

'How?' I snapped. Suddenly Jon's feelings towards me were of vital importance. 'How can you tell?'

'He's always asking about you.'

I shrugged. 'So? Big deal. Why wouldn't he? We go back a long way. You live with me and work with him; it's natural that he'd ask you about me. Who do you expect to ask about me? The postman?' I snorted to show her how absurd her suggestion was.

'So why's he asking?'

I rolled my eyes. 'He's a nice guy. We've got a history. Doesn't mean we fancy one another. And given the way things ended with him and Stuart at A SPACE, I mean, he can hardly ring me at work to ask me how I am, can he? Stuart would go ballistic. No, you are totally off the track. Jon and I are just great friends, end of story.'

'Plus he always goes on about your "great eye".'

'My eye?' I clamped my hand to my face – was there something wrong with one of my eyes? I began to panic. 'What's the matter with my eye?'

Alice pulled my hand away. 'Taste,' she explained. 'He's always saying stuff like "Saskia would love that", and then he sort of gazes off into the distance. I can just tell. It's obvious. He definitely likes you.'

Emmanuel was suddenly the last thing on my mind. I needed to know more about this Jon fancying me theory but at the same time I didn't want to let on to Alice that I cared two pins, so I shrugged my shoulders and feigned disinterest.

'Whatever,' I sighed, looking bored out of my mind. I may even have yawned. I began to pick at the laces of one of her blades. 'I mean, it doesn't matter, does it? Even if he does fancy me, I'd never be interested. Not after how he treated Stuart.'

'You loathe Stuart.'

'So? I loathe dogs. Doesn't mean I approve of people mistreating them.'

'True,' she said, turning another glass into a chimney stack. I got the feeling she'd lost interest in the conversation about Jon herself. Thing was, I was suddenly v. interested.

'So, then, I'm glad that little misconception's sorted,' I told her primly, folding my arms and sounding like my mother does when she's driven me up the wall and forced me to submit to going down to Horsham for Sunday lunch.

'Well, that's all right then,' Alice agreed as the smoke coiled out of her glass. 'Because I think he's started seeing someone else.'

I waved the smoke away as if it was really bothering me. Seeing someone else? My inner voice screamed out in pain. I'm surprised the whole bar didn't hear it. It certainly felt as if every eye in the room was on me. One minute I was digesting that Jon might actually fancy me, and then, just as I was more or less adjusting to the idea, it was snatched away from me.

'Seeing someone else? Who?'

She shrugged. 'Dunno. Just a hunch, really.'

'Not that I care obviously,' I told her as the bar began to crowd in on me. It felt as if the whole place was crushing me.

I had a sudden desire to get out of there, an irresistible urge to run out into heavy traffic. I was only holding myself together because I was afraid of people staring at me. I pinched some more bar snacks from another table while they weren't looking and went about repressing my emotions with food.

Alice shook her head and blew a cloud of smoke over me. I coughed ostentatiously. She'd always smoked cigars. Cohibas when she could get them, but mostly horrid el cheapos. But she only ever smoked one or two a day, which used to infuriate me. Not that I smoked at all, but I liked to pride myself on the fact that if I were to smoke, I would go at it with all guns blazing.

I'd be one of those desperate addicts you see at the cinema who charge out into the street at the intermission for a fag. Or those people on planes who get caught in the toilet (covered head to foot in nicotine patches) chuffing away on a Camel.

I'd light up as soon as I woke up and fall asleep with one sticking out of the side of my mouth like a true profligate.

I'd probably even accessorise my habit with jewel-encrusted cigarette cases and Dunhill lighters, and maybe even take to drinking whisky on the rocks and writing long postmodern novels about the decline of immorality in W11.

And when I saw *No Smoking* signs, I'd go absolutely berserk and scream incomprehensibly about the nanny state until someone stuck me with a Valium hypodermic. I'd collect on-the-spot no-smoking-zone fines like Ferrari drivers collect speeding tickets – with pride. Other smokers would marvel at my mettle and set their standards by me.

I would be the It girl of smokers everywhere. Cigarette companies would be lining up to have me on their ads – like a sort of new millennium Marlboro girl.

What I hate are the oh, so cool, low-tar cigarette smokers. The ones who haven't really got the lungs for the real thing; the ones who smoke for image alone; the ones who smoke 'Lights'. That's not smoking – that's posing!

Then I remembered that Jon smoked Lights.

He used to smoke roll-ups, which is v. cool. He once told me that he wished he could give up but lacked restraint. He'd tried to give up with Stuart years ago when Stuart decided that the gallery should be a smoke-free zone. Stuart had used the patches but Jon refused, saying it seemed too mad to get the drug without the fun. He'd settled for smoking Lights – which were also v. cool at the time.

Jon and I used to laugh at Stuart's restraint, although since Jon left A SPACE, Stuart has started smoking again like his life depends on it.

I've never been really good at restraint, but that's OK because Albert told me that it isn't a really evolved quality. Albert has no restraint whatsoever, which is why he makes such a great cutter.

My brother Martin was brilliant at restraint – eerily so, actually. It wasn't easy growing up with a brother who only ever ate one square of his Dairy Milk chocolate bar a day. *One square.*

When you think about it, it's amazing that my parents didn't put him out on the hillside or offer him up for scientific tests or something. Surely it goes against the genetic code to approach a bumper bar of chocolate with a one-piece-at-a-time attitude. It's the stuff of *The X Files* really, something you imagine aliens who want to take over the world doing.

Every Christmas we were given a bumper block of choc-olate each, and mine used to go in the one day, usually squeezed in between pudding and Christmas cake.

Martin started his block on Boxing Day and sometimes even later – New Year's Day one year. The suspense was horrendous. I remember biting my nails to the quick with anticipation.

Once opened, he could make the bar stretch through most of January. It wasn't because he was mean or anything; the opposite, in fact. He always shared everything, including the chocolate. But only ever one square.

Albert said that he must have been a control freak, a sadist who loved power, but if that was true he was going the wrong way about it. Personally I always thought he should have used his chocolate rations to his advantage, like prisoners do in jail with cigarettes, to stop other prisoners raping them in the shower or to get first turn at the slops bucket.

Martin might have bargained his way into the better of our two rooms if he had been wily. I was a sucker for chocolate.

As it was, Martin became a Buddhist and went to live in Cambridge and now he doesn't even bother to go home for Christmas to get his chocolate ration. Mum stopped buying them for him, which was a great tragedy because for a few years there I was getting double rations, while Mum was still hopeful that he'd get sick of lentil stew and sneak out to Sussex for turkey with all the trimmings.

Now she says stuff like, 'Never mind, at least he seems happy.'

'So do people who run off to join the Moonies,' I tell her. But my mother is resigned to men leaving; she thinks it's inevitable that they will run away. My dad did. Mum thinks of men as delicate, highly strung creatures who need everything just so or they break out in phobias.

My father hasn't been seen since he went for a walk in

the Himalayas ten years ago. As far as we know he's still up there, walking out on his Nepalese wives every time they breed. He wrote once asking Mum to send his stuff and she did, along with twelve new pairs of socks. Which sort of said a lot about both of them, really.

The bar was really filling up now with the after-work crowd. City blokes in their red braces, designer suits and colourful ties out for a brag. Estate agents in their off-the-rack suits and striped shirts doing a last bit of networking before they went home to Putney.

I wanted to ask Alice if there was any chance that Jon would drop in after the gallery closed, but I couldn't see how I could slip a remark like that in without kick-starting the Jon-fancying-me conversation again. Even though I wasn't in the least bit interested in the Jon-fancying-me concept (course not), I couldn't face hearing about how Jon was fancying someone else now. Crazy really, because I didn't feel anything like that for Jon. Course not.

It occurred to me that maybe I was one of those madly possessive friends who couldn't bear it when her best friend dates other girls, like Julia Roberts in *My Best Friend's Wedding*.

Whatever: I really couldn't have coped with Jon walking in arm in arm with another girl, especially a gorgeous size ten with a tremendous career. I really couldn't cope with that. Nor could I take my eyes off the door.

I was relating to the dogs in bandannas tethered to seats outside. I could see them licking the tops of discarded bottles of designer beer and scanning the crowds mournfully, hoping against hope that someone would come and claim them and take them home.

The music had been bumped up several decibels and we now had to shout to make ourselves heard. One of the nerdy girls sitting beside us had taken her top off to expose a rather rubbery torso and a Marks & Spencer's bra.

We'd ordered and reordered, and our table was getting quite crowded with empties. The Australian girl with the *Baywatch* body had changed shifts with a hunky German guy, who was almost enough to take my mind off my sorrows.

But only almost.

I'd read an article about how German women would rather sleep with blow-up dolls than with German men. I felt sorry for him and gave him a look that said, 'I would sleep with you, Klaus, if I wasn't feeling so bloody tragic.'

A couple of people were beginning to stare at our table, possibly because they'd just realised who was nicking their bar snacks, but their attention made me feel a bit paranoid. It made me want to go home, and I was still terrified that Jon and his new girl would come striding through the doors. I couldn't cope if they came over to our table and said 'Hi!' as if nothing was wrong. Alice didn't look remotely in the mood to leave, though. I decided to try to make her as desperate to leave as me.

'Stop doing that,' I hissed at her. She was onto her second cigar and still blowing smoke into the empty glasses on the table. 'Everyone's staring.'

'So?' she said, looking up.

Telling Alice she was being noticed was the wrong tack, I realised. She loves being noticed. Drunk or sober, Alice is an attention-seeker extraordinaire. As close as you can get to an exhibitionist without taking her knickers off in public basically.

'They think you're dumping me,' I whispered, trying another angle.

'What are you on about?' she asked, slightly confused.

I whispered in her ear. 'I think everyone thinks we're a lesbian couple.'

I knew this would get Alice moving. She was always worried about blokes thinking she was a lesbian and not bothering to try to chat her up.

'Why would you think of something like that?' she asked, checking out the odd stares we were getting.

'Well, look at them, they're staring at us. They see me upset, they see you disinterested and blowing smoke into the glasses. They naturally think we're having a lover's tiff.' I was having to hiss loudly over the noise of the music, which meant that quite a few more heads turned in our direction.

'You're getting paranoid, no one's looking, and anyhow,' she said, sweeping the room with her eyes, 'let them think what they want, there's no one worth bothering with here. Maybe you should have another drink,' she suggested.

'Maybe we should go,' I said, checking out the way everyone in the bar was clutching their bowls of snacks to their chests.

'No one will ever look at you in this place, of that you can be sure,' Alice reassured me. 'This is the best area of London to come to if you don't want to be noticed. Believe me. I always come here if I don't want to be noticed.'

I looked at her quizzically. I couldn't imagine Alice not wanting to be noticed; she was always the centre of attention. That was where Alice and I differed. When I was a kid, I always used to complain to my mother about people staring at me. 'Oh, don't be so vain,' she used to say. 'Who'd want to look at you? Chance would be a fine thing.'

Even when I was in the school play and turned to my mother for words of comfort to get me over those first-night nerves, she'd scoff. 'Why do you want to be nervous about going on stage? You? You're only one of the donkeys. Why, everyone'll be looking at Mary. No one will even notice *you*.'

Attention was something that happened to other girls, girls of exceptional beauty. Girls like my sister Rebecca basically. Seven years older than me and now married and living in Richmond with her merchant banker husband and three gorgeous children, my sister was the apple of my mother's eye.

It was only of minor comfort to me that Rebecca's life now revolved around planning Jeremy's meals and supervising their Croatian nanny on how not to shake the baby.

Throughout my childhood Rebecca had been the star, the one destined for great things, whereas I was marked down on my report as 'satisfactory'. Is there any crueller remark? It was never thought that I might do well, and even when I graduated from college with honours, my mother was unimpressed.

'Your sister didn't need a degree, of course,' she never tired of reminding me. 'She was able to marry well thanks to her looks.'

My mother saw marrying well as the ultimate accomplishment for a woman. As far as she was concerned, feminism had never happened. Looks were everything. 'You're pretty in your way,' my mother conceded whenever she'd made me deeply depressed about my looks. When she'd finally got me to stop sobbing, she always added, 'But you'll never turn heads.'

The List of Things I want to Forget

1　First time I went 'all the way'.
2　First time I fell in love and made a total fool of myself by sending shameful, undignified notes to a boy who pinned them up in his dorm.
3　First time I got drunk (see number one).
4　Second time I drank and threw up on my boyfriend, precluding a second sexual experience (see numbers 1 and 2 above).
5　Going to work for Stuart Dumass.
6　Being a bridesmaid at my sister Rebecca's wedding.
7　Not going to work for Jon Tashco.
8　Developing a taste for fatty foods.
9　Sleeping with Emmanuel.
10　All the times I've ever believed a lie.

Several too many Bloody Marys later, I proved my mother wrong. By then every head in the bar was turned towards me. Eat your womb out with envy, Rebecca!

With my unfocused eyes hidden behind my Gucci sunglasses, my shirt tied up under my bust revealing a bare midriff and my skirt drifting up to expose my knickers, I was dancing on a centre table. Invincible, inscrutable and utterly gorgeous, if only my mother could have seen me.

'Don't you think you should get down now, Saskia?' Alice pleaded above the din of the smoke-filled bar.

'I'm having a fantastic time!' I told her, readjusting my sunglasses and doing another star kick to the wild applause of the late-night crowd, mostly a bunch of shaven-headed artists I'd turned down for shows at the gallery where I worked.

The estate agents and the City boys had all gone home to the civilised society of Fulham and Putney, where the risk of table dancers was still relatively slim.

I felt the table totter, steadied myself and bowed flamboyantly. I was a star and I knew it. The world was my oyster and I was its pearl.

Oh, dear.

'I need another drink!' I yelled, holding my satin shoe out for a refill.

'God, Saskia, you're destroying those shoes,' Alice admonished.

'Are you mad?' I shrieked. 'You can't destroy shoes that have survived since the 1880s, they're, they're, they're on another plane. Another dimension. They live among us, but they are not of us,' I declared, getting into my Roman Emperor stride. 'These shoes have been created as a sign that there is more to life than mere flesh and blood.'

OK, so it wasn't one of my best oratorial moments, but it was only temporary madness. When you're getting over a man, dancing on bar tables and drinking from satin shoes and generally making a fool of yourself is all part of the healing process, as any post-millennium girl will tell you.

'You'll kill yourself,' Alice warned, grabbing my arm as the table dipped dangerously. 'Come on, let's get going now. It's late.'

'Late? Late? It's not even closing time, you killjoy,' I jeered.

The audience backed me up with a cacophony of hoots, whistles and cheers.

'Come on, Sass, do that drinking thing with your shoe again!' someone with green stubbly hair called out.

'Yeah, that was brilliant!' agreed another of my adoring fans, nudging his nonplussed girlfriend in the ribs. By the way she was looking at me, she no doubt concurred with Alice that it was time for the dancing blonde in sunglasses to leave the bar and never return.

'Come on, you're going to feel awful tomorrow,' Alice hissed.

I looked at her like she was a Tory canvassing for votes in Islington. Besides, I was thinking, who was Alice to lecture me on my hangover prospects anyway? This was a woman who carried illegal quantities of Alka-Seltzer in her handbag, just in case. Hangovers were part of Alice's life of hard drinking, hard smoking and hard loving.

A bloke in a tight retro suit standing on a chair on the other side of the room was blowing kisses at me. He had about fifty studs in a face only a mother could love, but I was sufficiently encouraged by his sense of occasion to blow a few kisses back.

'See, my audience loves me!' I told her, pointing out my studded fan.

'Yeah, right! This crowd would love Margaret Thatcher if she came in here and hitched her dress up high enough. I don't know what we're doing here when we both have to get up in the morning. I'm going, and if you've got an unpickled brain cell left, you'll come with me,' she informed me, drowning her cigar butt meaningfully in my now liquid shoe.

Alice is a New Yorker, incorrigibly sensible in all things, except when it comes to shoes (Vivienne Westwood platforms, even for work) and men (she can pick them, like *not*) alcohol and cigars. OK, maybe not so sensible, but who wants to take the advice of a sensible person?

I'd only known her for a few months when she answered my ad on the noticeboard at Jon's new gallery for a flatmate. By then she had also secured the job as his new assistant.

What struck me as special about Alice was that even in the throes of a break-up, she maintained a truly awesome grip on her cognitive processes. Alice has got something that my mother recognised I would never have from day one: common sense. For starters, she knew better than all the retro-suited wannabes in Cantaloupe that night what that flimsy bar table would hold. And it wasn't a nine-stone, five-foot-seven bottle blonde with a newly discovered talent for star kicks.

I tried to focus on her and give her a half-decent reply as the room swam around me.

'Well? Are you coming?' she pressed, pulling on my skirt.

My response was a spectacular spin kick which I'd seen a guy in *Starlight Express* do on television. It was quite easy really, you just throw yourself into mid-air and toss your arms and legs about the place madly and smile.

The last thing I remember was the crescendo of applause as the world collapsed from underneath me. After that, the What I Want from a Relationship list flashed before my eyes and then everything went black.

What I Want from a Relationship

1 The right side of the bed and at least half the duvet.
2 Excitement, humour, passion and adoration. Natch.
3 Fantasy. I hope this doesn't sound shallow, but size does matter.
4 A man who understands that cellulite is a woman's equivalent to penis size. As in, I'll tell you that yours is huge, you tell me that I haven't got any – easy.
5 When I tell you I don't want you to make a fuss over Valentine's Day, anniversaries, birthdays, etc. that's because I don't want you to think that I'm shallow. Obviously it would be v. shallow of you to take me at face value.
6 Don't ever admit to equating PMT with unreasonable behaviour.
7 This point is optional but highly desirable. Let me catch you gazing lovingly down on me when I wake up.
8 Give up all interest in sport. Try saying stuff like, 'Who is Gazza, anyway?' when another guy tries to discuss football with you.
9 Press tokens of your affection on me. Poetry is fine too, although a blue box with white ribbon is preferable.
10 Commitment. Not as in marriage, but as in let's invest more in this thing than the cost of a box of condoms.

I woke up in bed the next morning with the list stuck to my face where I'd slept on it. A quick look at the clock confirmed my worst fear: I was an hour late for work. More alarmingly, the sun hadn't come up yet. Was this Armageddon? Had the world's arsenals of nuclear weapons finally been unleashed?

Actually no, I discovered after looking in the mirror. I was still wearing my sunglasses from the night before and not much else, now that I looked, apart from a suspender belt and a solitary stocking which had dribbled down my leg and was now clinging for dear life to my foot. Glued there by congealed Bloody Mary. V. Sally Bowles.

It felt like an ashtray was lodged in my mouth and all my muscles felt like someone had given them Chinese burns. My head was pounding with the ferocity of shame more than pain, though. Unfortunately I could remember the night before in unnecessarily vivid detail and I scolded my brain cells for their determination to survive. Had I really danced on a table? Ouch!

The stench of my shoes still sodden with Bloody Marys made me gag, dislodging every best-forgotten memory of how I had been indecorously shovelled into a taxi, and how the driver had assisted Alice in getting me into the flat.

There was a particularly nasty image which my synapses offered up, of me clinging to the cab driver's leg and promising him that, if he helped me onto the coffee table, I would show him my Margot Fonteyn impersonation. Then I remembered that the cab driver had seemed amenable to the suggestion and Alice had offered him ten pounds to ignore my invitation.

I struggled to stand, finding support from my clothes rack, which, for the first time in our long relationship, didn't collapse into a broken heap on the floor. There was a note pinned to my door from Alice telling me there were hangover cures in the bathroom, and a list of instructions on how to use the espresso machine.

This info took a while to filter through to the relevant section of my brain. At the bottom of the list she had written *Today is the Day – New York or Die!* Death didn't seem like such an unappealing notion.

Alice and I had made a pact one drunken evening when we'd first met that we'd have a holiday in New York together. It was easy for her – she had a boss who believed in the Geneva Convention.

Not that I didn't dream of visiting the Big Apple, but the actuality of pinning Stuart down for the purpose of saying something that would make him want to murder me just didn't appeal in the cool light of sobriety.

I hated letting Alice down, I really did, but what else could I do? I guess I was hoping that if I prevaricated long enough she'd get bored of waiting and go alone or take someone else. She was from New York, for God's sake, I mean it wasn't like I was abandoning her on a package tour to Cuba or anything.

The sunlight was streaming in through the broken blinds of our Notting Hill flat, which pissed me off no end and brought out the sarcastic worst in me. Brilliant! It was May, I'd been waiting for the sun to appear for months and with the typical bloody-mindedness of the English weather, it decided to choose a red-letter hangover day to turn up the UV to retina-burning intensity.

I threw my pillow at the blinds and broke another few slats.

Half an hour later, I was emptying the contents of our bathroom cabinet into my system, including one of Alice's suppositories by accident. She's into detoxing and cleansing her system almost as much as she's into polluting and abusing it. I mean, the girl's got problems. She has enemas and colonic irrigations like I have manicures and facials, as a means of spoiling herself.

After a few wrong turns I eventually managed to stagger into the kitchen. Normally the kitchen and I are relative strangers to one another, and so it was natural that I should be momentarily stunned at how clean it was; hygienic almost.

I'm more your bathroom/bedroom kind of girl, content to leave the kitchen side of life to others. Just the same, it was an emergency and Alice had set up the espresso machine for me, darling that she is. Believe me, I'm not exaggerating when I say I would never have made it down to the tube station without that coffee.

I somehow managed to dress myself, choosing an outfit that would hide the largest possible expanse of my anatomy in one go – purdah would have been ideal. After throwing the best part of my wardrobe around my room, I settled on a long, flowing, white cheesecloth thing I'd bought last summer at Hyper Hyper on High Street Kensington. I teamed this choice with regulation Israeli army boots. Yes: it was definitely a 'dodging-stones-on-the-hot-streets-of-Bethlehem' kind of day, I told my reflection. 'You said it,' my reflection replied.

Like most people suffering with hangovers, humanity was my enemy that morning. The new immorality dictated that someone was going to *get it* and for better or worse I chose Jake, the bloke that begs down by the station.

I know that unless you live in Notting Hill and make a habit of getting to know your local itinerant population, you probably don't know Jake. But believe me, you know his type. There was no one who deserved this mood more than Jake.

He lives in Ladbroke Grove and does the morning and evening shift at Notting Hill tube, collecting change from guilt-ridden middle-class commuters. Notting Hill is an area that is positively smoggy with conscience. Think restaurants you can never get a booking in; think exposed brickwork, terracotta-painted walls; think young designers, media types and actors; think oversized white sofas and think conscience – lots of conscience. That's my area.

Jake's about my age. He studied art for, like, five minutes at Goldsmith's when I was there and I hated him then and I hate him now. He was one of those guys who smoked too much pot at a point of high hormonal activity and caught the millennium bug. You know, that disease where people think the world is going to end any day and so what's the point of aspiring to anything when we're all going to be eating cockroaches anyway. That's Jake's theory. Sometimes I even believe him if he gets me on a low point in my cycle.

Jake is just one of those people I have always hated, though; I bet if I went to one of those past life experts they'd tell me I have hated Jake for thousands of years. We were probably hating one another in Ancient Egypt. It certainly felt like that. He was everything I don't want in a man and then some.

Recently he's started going out with the girl who sells hair accessories down the market. I'm always telling her she can do better – like I'm someone who'd know!

That morning, Jake was pretending to whimper with cold even though it was a pretty gorgeous day for folk without hangovers. He was wearing a thick scarf, donkey jacket, woollen gloves sans fingers and a beanie. Any self-respecting beggar would throw the cliché book at him for that outfit.

When he saw me he stopped his whining and said, 'Mate saw you at Cantaloupe last night. Not bad legs, he reckons.' Then he leered suggestively and pushed his grimy nose into my face.

I couldn't think of anything clever to say in my fragile state, so I just emptied the rag that he collects his change in and felt my hangover lift slightly as the coins scattered noisily down the station steps. Sometimes it takes the catalyst of a hangover to do something you've wanted to do for years.

'Hey, why'd you do that?' he whimpered. Only it was a fairly loud whimper, more a stage whimper, so that other passers-by could hear. If there's one thing that Jake loves, it's playing to the crowd.

Feeling a rush of new immorality coming on, I grinned. 'Because you're scum,' I told him.

The bloke who sells the *Big Issue* near Oxfam across the street clapped. Jake is about as friendless a beggar as you could imagine. There is a growing sense of bitterness among local beggars because Jake isn't actually homeless: in fact he collects the dole and lives in an ultra-beige flat with Sky TV.

A woman who mans the paper stand made a wanking sign with her hand while Jake bent over to gather his coins. Basically all the locals hate Jake because he pisses outside their shops when they're not looking. The station stinks with Jake's piss. He justifies it by saying it adds atmosphere and makes people more aware of his plight.

A woman in a navy two-piece helped him pick up his coins. She looked at me like I'd just kicked a puppy, and, being the exponent of the new immorality that I am, I smiled at her proudly.

By choice, I'm fairly unclear about the details of the rest of my journey into work. There's not a lot about a journey on the Central line that anyone would want to remember, really.

I usually get into an argument with someone who thinks they can ride into Bond Street station on my foot, and this morning was no different. 'Do you want to move it, buddy?' I asked the guy in my best North American drawl. I got this from Alice. Londoners are always really intimidated by cross Americans on the tube, especially if you wear a red beret. They think you belong to a vigilante group and they'll do anything you say. Sometimes if the train's super-full I'll say, 'Move along, will yu?' and it's brilliant – they pack themselves up one end of the carriage, all nervous. Sometimes I think they're going to say 'Don't shoot, *please*!'

I lay low most of the morning playing Tomb Raider and wishing I had an arsenal like Lara Croft. Some of the time I just sat there holding my head in my hands, moaning softly and watching my breath mist up on the screen. I made a list of things I was never going to do again. Top of the list was drink.

No one came in all morning and so there was no reason to move from my post. Which was probably why I kept getting pins and needles down my body.

Around one o'clock I was still putting off making body movements out of fear of kicking my headache back into action or worse still, bumping into my boss. It was near enough two o'clock when his shadow fell over my *Big Issue*. Gulp.

I swallowed hard, clicked my justification process onto autopilot and prayed that I would self-immolate or that an enemy power would launch a scud missile at A SPACE. I was about to go into one of my thousand and one excuses as to why I should be allowed to exist, when the hateful bastard announced that I could have a *lunch break*.

'Huh?'

'Lunch break. You know, food, eat?' He made eating

movements with his hands in case I'd forgotten the concept.

What new form of torture is this? I wanted to ask. First
an afternoon off and now lunch, all within a two-day period.
Had he gone back on the LSD?

I put this to him.

'Don't be silly. You have to eat something, Saskia.'

I cast the paper aside and looked up into the evil green
eyes of my employer, Stuart Dumass. 'Let me get this clear.
You want me to walk out in that sunshine and take a lunch
break?'

'I won't need you here for a while,' he explained, staring
into the street. 'So you may as well go and catch a bit of
sunshine. It's a fantastic day out there.' He pointed through
the wall of glass that separated us from the outside world
like Moses directing his people to the Holy Land. Then he
smiled down on me as if it was the most natural thing to do
in the world to turn your employee out for lunch.

Despite my personal feelings towards my boss, all my
friends are really impressed that I work for him. I try to
tell them that he's the budding boot-camp commandant of
the West End contemporary art world but they ignore me.
'You mean you work for *The* Stuart Dumass? Wow! How
glamorous!' they caw.

It was all true. I, Saskia Williams, curatorial wannabe,
eternally waiting for that big break, the one that will catapult
me into the pages of *Vogue* and other English glossies as
London's greatest gallery girl ever, the break that would
have the Groucho Club begging me to join. I work for the
Stuart Dumass of social pages fame.

Stuart was the man who had discovered Andrew Farn,
the lad who took the art world by storm in the early nineties
exhibiting X-rays of his groin to great financial acclaim.
There have been a score of *artfant terribles* discovered by
Stuart since, most of them Turner Prize winners, but alas

I hadn't had the chance to choose one of them. Not a single one.

He'd listen to my opinions and ideas for shows and mutter something about how these decisions were dependent on a number of factors, and totally ignore me. I was, in short, his dogsbody, his run-around, his shit-kicker.

Stuart had promised me when I came to work for him that I would be in charge of curating a third of the shows. Needless to say, that promise had never materialised. When Jon was here of course it was all so much fun that I didn't have time to dwell on mundane issues like my future, but career prospects are very important to a girl closing in on thirty. Especially when the boyfriend shares have plummeted so drastically.

I guess I had to face the fact that I was never going to become one of those women who lunch. Not that I'd ever really counted on it, but it was one of those images that occasionally popped into my head in idle moments. The thought that someone might want to 'keep' me, as opposed to chuck me.

Lugging canvases around a gallery and sucking up to buyers is not what I'd dreamt of when I graduated from art school. Back then I was planning to become a curator, immortalised by my stable of artists – all gorgeous young men with a keen sense of personal hygiene. We are talking fantasy, natch. In idle moments I dreamed of these drop-dead sexy artists clustered at my feet, artists who longed to get close to me but satisfied themselves with worshipping me from the distance of our professional relationship.

Vogue would always want to write about me, I would be asked to judge the Turner Prize. I would be named one of the most influential women in British art, dwarfing the very artists whose names I made. The usual stuff.

Working at this gallery began as a stopgap measure, taken to placate my bank manager whom I was trying to persuade to lend me the money to start my own gallery. Six years on, my bank manager was an MP, no doubt enjoying lucrative cash-for-questions perks, and I was still in this shitty job.

Now that I'd broken up with Emmanuel, I'd decided that the time was right to push out the career envelope and start my future as a curator. Forget men: I was going to become a serious career woman, a definer of trends, a cutter of edges. Only thing was, I didn't have the guts to tell my boss.

Talking of whom, Stuart was still staring out into the street like a zombie. 'Right then, er . . . lunch it is,' I said, grasping the nettle. 'Can I, um, get you anything at all?' I asked.

He looked down at me with what I can only imagine was a smile of suppressed contempt. The feeling was mutual. Stuart was down on my hit list; in fact he had several entries.

Regardless of my inside info on Stuart, there are those in London who persist in adoring him. I suppose in a good light he didn't look too bad: tall, dark hair, sexy-as-hell jawline and green eyes. On close inspection, yes, I would have to say he was handsome, as long as you didn't get too close and cut yourself on his razor-sharp sarcasm.

'No, just go,' he said, sneaking in a withering look at my footwear. 'We don't seem to be busy just at the moment.'

Huh. Stuart is the master of euphemism. Since this latest show went up, we couldn't even bribe passers-by to enter. With the offer of escape on the horizon I didn't argue. I grabbed my sunglasses and ran, faster than a crowd of art groupies who have heard that Damien Hirst is signing autographs.

The List of Qualities I Require in order to Succeed in the Twenty-first Century

1   The capability to think global, ie must learn how to use A to Z.
2   Flexibility/high mobility/resourcefulness, ie ability to take the District line if circumstances dictate.
3   Seek endless career growth. Be prepared to work Saturdays.
4   Ability to access needed information in real time – must be cyberpuss.
5   Be dynamic, fast-paced and eager for new challenges, ie refuse to make the coffee.
6   Adapt rapidly to new situations/new people, etc.
7   Develop a sense of urgency about future goals.
8   Embrace innovation and new technologies, ie mobile phone, etc.
9   Be high-tech but remain high-touch, ie be prepared to shake hands if situation dictates.
10 Keep nails neat and well filed, ie do not gnaw.

Out on the street in the twenty-five-degree heat, my brain fell in upon itself. The motherboard of my enthusiasm drive melted. Problem was, I didn't have the appropriate resource chip for challenges. I adapted too well to discomfort – God, I wouldn't be living in London if I didn't. I was too ready to accept second-best.

When push came to shove, my resources amounted to a knowledge of where to get the cheapest fifteen-denier tights in London and how to survive the tube during rush hour.

Instead of the rejuvenating romp through Selfridges cosmetics department I'd planned for myself, I ended up getting stuck in the doors between two security guards about to run off in pursuit of a shoplifter.

I was not their favourite person by the time they disentangled themselves from my billowing dress. V. embarrassing.

'Be Holly Golightly!' Albert was always advising. 'Think *Breakfast at Tiffany's!*' But it wasn't that easy. Especially since I'd been banned from the Bond Street branch of Tiffany's after inadvertently setting off their security system by using my nail file to open one of the glass cabinets.

I was just trying to save time!

All the staff were busy, so basically I thought I would help myself. But that's another story.

It just wasn't so easy being winsome and delightful without

the size six figure and flawless skin Audrey had at her disposal. It was going to be even less easy after my undignified wrestle with the security guys.

I had to face it, I was all of dynamic resources. And as for the ability to think global, forget it. I couldn't even envisage life outside of Notting Hill most of the time.

What I needed was an ego boost, a turbo-blast. I needed to make Emmanuel rue the day he'd chucked me – yes, that was it. I must make him suffer. I must make him squirm. I must ruin his belief in himself as sexually attractive, worthy of blow jobs, etc. – yes, that was more in keeping with the spirit of the new immorality.

As soon as I realised this, my self-esteem began to puff out its chest again. The most pressing thing in my life had become the search for something that would go with the fifties orange hessian shoes I'd bought on sale last month for a big party coming up at the Saatchi gallery.

Emmanuel was going to be there, and so looking good wasn't merely an option but an obligation. I read somewhere that if you focus on your heart's desire at the point of orgasm, it works like a kind of invocation.

I opted for the positive affirmation method instead. I would visualise walking into that party looking like a dream, all eyes upon me, a whisper hissing through the space as media people asked one another, 'Who is that delicious size ten?' PS: I was going to eat nothing but wheatgrass juice between now and then.

Seeing Emmanuel break down at the sight of my desirability and publicly weeping with remorse would surely give me the lift I needed.

Maybe I should start making positive affirmations about him pleading with me in front of everyone to have no-strings sex with him in the future. Of course, I would laugh hysterically in his face, but it would be nice to hear him beg.

The sticking point in this operation was a problem with shoes, though. Shoes have never come easy with me. Secretly I dream of flat shoes, but deep down I know that flat shoes are like woolly tights – v. comfy but the king of all turn-offs.

The shoes which were causing me the most problems were the orange hessian ones, about the worst combination imaginable, I know, but that was it. The shop owner on Golborne Road had told me they were 'to die for', and insisted they would go with 'absolutely anything'.

What she meant was anything orange and hessian, basically. A fruitless search around South Molton Street left me feeling flaccid in the hope stakes again; I couldn't even afford those price tags. Resigned to my fate, I began the trudge back to the gallery.

A bloke curled up in a sleeping bag asked me for some change, so I gave him one of the two cans of vodka and tonic I'd just bought. A bloke in a polyester pullover told me not to encourage him and I told him hotly that someone should have encouraged him not to wear that jumper.

I don't normally drink at work, but I thought I might be able to use the V&T's as a means of softening Stuart up for the New York holiday idea. But on second thoughts I didn't think I could face alcohol again, so my homeless friend was well pleased.

When I got back to A SPACE, Stuart was down in the storeroom doing one of his fastidious stocktakes. He told me to sit by the phone as he was expecting an important call. 'In your dreams,' I thought to myself – I mean, we hadn't exactly been inundated with enquiries about this latest show.

I briefly tortured the idea of confronting him with a request for my rightful holiday entitlement, telling myself that maybe it wasn't such an off-the-wall request. After all, hadn't he given me a lunch break and an afternoon off?

On the other hand, maybe he was seeing if he could do without me? Maybe he was merely warming up to fire me. Jobless and boyfriendless? The prospect terrified me. I decided to wait until he'd had his drink and went into the kitchenette area to prepare it.

Hidden in the little dark annexe where we had a drinks fridge for punters and a small sink, I set about trying to break into the can. After a lot of nail-breaking and cursing, I did finally manage to pull off the tab but then someone walked into the gallery.

On hearing the door buzz I dropped everything and skipped out as best as I could in my Israeli army-issue boots. The possibility of a sale put a bit of a spring in my step – or maybe I was just glad to put off my confrontation with Stuart that little bit longer.

No, I was desperate for a sale. Although I was paid a meagre wage, I relied on my one per cent commission for essentials, ie, make-up, clothes, the odd taxi, entertainment and that most daunting expense of all – sundries.

Looking around at the hopeless canvases leaning against the wall, though, I didn't hold out much hope for a sale. Symptomatic of all Stuart's latest finds, this show was called *Experiences in White* and believe me, the paintings were even less inspiring than the title.

'Hello, Saskia darling!' my mother called over the cacophonous clunk, clunk, clunk of her heels on the stripped-wood floor. It was often remarked upon that the acoustics of A SPACE were more intimidating than the prices.

Not that I wasn't over the moon to see her, it was just that she always made me feel like I was a middle-aged spinster rather than the late twenties party girl I tried to project.

We kissed. She mentioned a new series of lines around my eyes and told me that white made me look pasty. She then went on to cluck about Rebecca's new kitchen and Jeremy's latest promotion and how, while it would be mad for me to hope for Rebecca's level of achievement, I might perhaps do something with my hair.

'The problem with my hair, Mum, is that I've done too much with it. Even my hairdresser has started to admit that there may well be nothing more he can do. It's been bleached, crimped, machine-rolled, tinted, tainted and turned inside out from the roots.'

My mother began to look agitated. When I start speaking my mind she gets flustered.

'Who's the artist?' she asked, looking around the space, slightly disgusted as if she was worried about stepping in something nasty. I'd taken her to a Piero Manzoni exhibition at the Serpentine Gallery once – you know, the guy who exhibited his poo in the sixties? Ever since then, my mother has turned up her nose at the very idea of contemporary art. Rebecca, of course, has a house full of ancient watercolours by RA blokes, and wouldn't come to A SPACE if we gave out free manicures.

I gave Mum's tweedy shoulders a hug and took her over to one of the paintings. 'His name's Jeff Hewit, as in son of Lord Rupert Hewit,' I explained.

'Oh?' she said, slightly warming to them. My mother is the ultimate snob. I could see her mind ticking over and I knew she was wondering how old this son of Lord Hewit's was, and whether he was married, and whether there was any chance he could be prevailed upon to fancy her pasty daughter, who was nowhere near as good-looking as her sister and indeed was riddled with lines around the eyes.

'Awful, aren't they?' I said, trying to reassure her that it was all right to hate them – not that my mum needs reassurance to hate anything. 'That one by the door is entitled "White Mood Swing".'

She gazed at the painting for a bit and then cast her eyes about the room doubtfully. 'But is this Hewit man nice, dear?'

'He's old and wizened and extremely married, and to top it off, would you believe it, he's gay,' I lied.

'They all look the same to me,' she sniffed, pretending she hadn't heard me. My mother doesn't appreciate her schemes being uncovered.

'That's the point,' I explained as I took her arm and led her round the twenty or so flat, white, identically sized canvases leaning along the walls. 'They're an ironic statement on the art world.'

'Aren't you going to hang them?' she asked. 'They look so abandoned leaning on the walls like that, as if the artist has just run off and left them to dry.'

'Philistine, Mum! Wash your mouth out, the artist would die. Anyway, there's nothing to dry – they're blank canvases. He thinks they look more *nascent* that way!'

'Are they awfully good, then?' she enquired politely, with the bliss of the truly ignorant. 'Is this the sort of art you want to curate?'

I was surprised that she even remembered the word. Normally my mother brushes off the idea of me having a career. She doesn't want me to get distracted from the main aim of finding a suitable husband. 'Oh, my God,' the paranoid within me cried – did this mean that even my mother was resigned to having a spinster for a daughter?

'No, Mum, they're crap,' I told her firmly. 'And not just any old crap either – dated crap. I mean, think about it, he couldn't even be contemporary in his choice of crap. Not that anyone is going to tell His Highness Jeff Hewit that. Not when his father was the late, great Lord Rupert Hewit, England's most notorious artist. Died in a pool of his own vomit.'

'His what, dear?' she asked. She always liked me to repeat disgusting words twice so that she could chastise me about being unladylike, but just then Stuart walked in and asked, 'Who left this opened can on the sink?'

My mother and I spun around to face him. I just managed to smother a giggle – but only just. His frown was so fierce that his chin was all dimpled up like cellulite. Seeing me with what he thought might be a client, he did a double take and pulled his facial muscles into a smile.

'I'm sorry, I didn't realise you were with someone,' he said, all charm and politeness. 'Can I offer you a cup of coffee, tea? A glass of wine, perhaps?'

I fixed him with one of my 'piss off, I'm with a client' smiles, but to no avail – Mum had decided to have her say. It's something they put in the water in West Sussex, I think.

'Not for me, thank you. Stuart, isn't it? We met briefly a couple of years back. I'm Saskia's mother. I won't be staying long, just giving her some mail. Saskia's been telling me about her ideas for curating a summer show, and I must say she could do worse than this miserable Hewit fellow. I can't believe that he won't even bother to hang the things. Just because he's the son of somebody or other, he thinks he doesn't have to bother. I blame the mother. If one of my children . . .'

That's my mum.

'Saskia's always been full of ideas – always, even as a little gel,' she added. 'Never much to look at, but my word she was keen on making her mark. Always full of energy. Her sister was the beauty, of course, but . . .'

I toyed briefly with the idea of charging across the gallery and snatching the V&T from Stuart's hands and sculling its contents down in front of them both. Mind you, nothing I did would surprise my mother.

'Oh, yes, Saskia's full of ideas,' he replied caustically. Stuart could strip paint with his sarcasm.

'It's good to see her so committed to art, even if her own artistic endeavours haven't flourished.' Rub it in, Mum. 'Commitment is so important, don't you think, Stuart?'

'Yes, I've thought Saskia should be committed,' he snarled.

Mum carried on blithely, moving from my failure as an

artist to my failure to get a career off the ground, to my failure to marry and then straight into her speech about how wonderful and ideal Rebecca was.

My mother was immune to sarcasm. Like embarrassment, it's one of the things you must give up if you want to become a pillar of Horsham high society. She beamed at me and then at Stuart. 'I think it's marvellous, your giving her a break.'

'Mum!' I pleaded, doing that trick where I roll my eyes back into my head and allow my tongue to spill down my chin. Mum knows this look well: it's a look I started giving her around the force-feeding-peas stage of our relationship. She pointed at me and laughed.

'Isn't she a trick?'

'A veritable bag thereof,' Stuart groaned, coming over towards us presumably for the purpose of ejecting my mother and possibly even me. He didn't look happy.

'She deserves a break, doesn't she, Stuart? Heaven knows, she's been unlucky enough with men. Though in my view she should push herself forward more. When I was young, I was peeling boys off my shoes. They simply threw themselves at me at the Conservative Club.' This I doubted, and said as much with a sigh. My mother threw me a glare.

'But then *I* was a beauty. My other daughter takes after me. Rebecca is a lovely-looking girl, simply lovely. Married well, naturally. I might have a photograph here in my bag somewhere.' She began to rummage around in her purse.

I was sure the only break Stuart thought I deserved was in the region of my neck. He made a sort of ugly, drowned-rat kind of spluttering sound as he turned to my mother. 'Excuse me, Mrs Williams, it's been charming to meet you, but I'm afraid—'

'Sutton,' Mum interrupted.

Stuart looked confused, which raised my will to live a bit.

'I'm sorry?' he stuttered, which is something I've never heard him do before.

'Sutton, my name is Sutton. Saskia reverted to my maiden name when she left home. Heaven knows why. Very silly, to my mind, and embarrassing, too . . .'

New York had never seemed so appealing.

'My father disappeared on a mountain,' I explained hastily before my mother went into the long justifications about the socks, etc. 'I didn't want to keep his name. It's so madly old-fashioned, don't you think, children being forced to take their father's name? And as much as Mum would love to stand around and get better acquainted, Stuart, I'm afraid she's going to have to dash.' I gave her a bit of a push.

'That's all right, dear, I have a half-hour before I'm meeting Lillian for coffee in Fortnum's,' she began before realising that it wasn't a suggestion but an order. Re-evaluating Stuart's expression of fury, she began to back towards the door. 'I'm only up for the day, I've just brought Saskia her mail.'

She thrust the mail into my hands, hugged me, promised to call and walked briskly out of *Experiences in White*, her sturdy two-inch heels clacking like a drum roll on the floorboards.

Right, I was thinking as I watched her splendid hourglass figure disappear. This is where the would-be curator with the blonde hair gets it. Better to get these things out of the way, I told myself, facing Stuart and baring the soft flesh of my neck to his grasp.

He just stood there, though, looking distracted and lost, as if in a trance. No doubt wondering if anyone would miss me if he buried me under the cement slabs in the stockroom.

'OK, I know I should have talked my curatorial plans over with you,' I stuttered. 'But it was your idea when I began here, and now that Jon's left, I thought you might appreciate my input. We can discuss it later, though; you'll probably need time to think about it. I know how distracted you've been since Jon left. And my idea for a holiday in New

York can wait too, if you like,' I threw in – may as well be throttled for a sheep as for a lamb.

'Jon?' he asked, looking completely lost.

'Tashco.'

'Oh,' he sighed. 'Listen Saskia, it all sounds great but I can't talk about this just now, I've got to catch an auction.'

And without so much as the merest hint of the homicide I'd been planning for myself, he ran off.

I stood there slack-jawed for a while, trying to work out what had happened. I mean, lucky break aside, this was very odd indeed, odder than odd, even. Normally Stuart would fly at a chance to have me at his mercy for a jolly good neck-wringing. Or a sacking. Maybe he hadn't taken my mad rantings in?

Besides which, I hadn't noticed anything about an auction in the appointment book. I was in that office sitting in his chair and going through his Filofax in a nanosecond.

As I suspected, there was nothing at all about auctions noted down, and that was weird. Let's get this much straight: Stuart is so anally retentive! he even writes his shopping list down in that diary.

Ever since he was audited two years ago, he even records things like, 'Bought loo rolls for gallery lav at Safeway – £4.99'. But for May 15, the slot between three and four was blank. Not a squiggle. Something was going on; my suspicions were aroused. Not that I'm a busybody or anything, but like most people in boring jobs, I was more than prepared to give suspicions about my boss full reign.

Sometimes it was hard to believe that Stuart and I had once been close. Years before, when I'd first come to work at A SPACE, we had all got along so well. But that changed when Jon left six months back. Before then we all used to stay late on Thursday nights drinking vodka martinis, having a laugh and talking about art into the wee hours.

Jon Tashco was always so much fun to work for – more a friend than a boss, really. The opposite of Stuart. Where Stuart was all stressed out and bossy, Tashco was laid-back and cool. About thirty-nine years old, he had the sort of chiselled features that got him column inches. He was one of the funniest, most madly eccentric men I've ever known. Not to mention a serious womaniser.

There was nothing Tashco wouldn't do for a good time.

Actually, generous to a fault, he wasn't madly practical and probably cost the gallery far more than he ever made for it, but Jon was the personality of A SPACE. When people thought A SPACE, they thought Jon Tashco and when he left, he took all the fun with him.

There was a chance once that Jon and I might even get it on years ago (under the effects of alcohol, natch). Once upon a time the art world of London had even taken bets. God knows, we'd flirted around the issue for years.

There had even been a bit of mutual groping one night when he'd driven me home, but that was the night before the big split with Stuart and neither of us had mentioned it since. That was why I was so sure that Alice was wrong about Jon fancying me. We'd been over that ground and it wasn't for us. End of story.

I still saw quite a bit of him around the art track (not that I'd ever tell Stuart that), especially now that Alice had gone to work for him. He was always at the Saatchi bashes and assorted gallery openings. The London contemporary art world was a bit of a fish pond, really.

Whenever Jon sees me, he always runs up and throws his arms around me like nothing's happened. The fact was, I still hadn't worked out what *had* happened between him and Stuart, as neither of them had seen fit to fill me in on the finer details of their acrimonious split.

There'd been clues that things were going wrong for months before the actual bust-up: bitching, snide comments, blaming one another for silly things and so on, but Stuart had always had a filthy temper. Jon and I just got on with it.

Eventually there was one momentous row. Artworks were flung – Petri dishes I think they were – spinning around the room like miniature flying saucers, carrying deadly cargoes of bacteria. One of them was unpromisingly labelled *Bubonic Plague*, although afterwards Gus, the artist, told me it was just beef bouillon.

Stuart had been totally gutted at the time of Jon's departure, especially when Jon got the boot in by taking most of our artists, leaving us with sad creatures like Jeff Hewit.

The weirdest thing was that Stuart didn't seem to want to do anything about it. He'd made absolutely zilch effort to find new blood. Apart from cracking the proverbial whip, I sometimes suspected that he'd given up on art. His heart just wasn't in it, which was another reason why I should be able to talk him into letting me take over part of the curating. If only I wasn't so bloody terrified.

Thinking about Jon had made me blush. I put my hand to my face and remembered what Alice had said last night about my feelings for him. Madness obviously, so then why was my pulse racing? Besides, he was seeing someone else now.

Not that I would ever date him after what he did to Stuart, anyway. I couldn't believe that Jon had done it at first, raided our stable, I mean. The two of them had been in partnership for years – they'd built this place up from scratch. They'd believed in their artists even when no one else had; fed their money, their houses and their cars into this gallery. Then when the rest of the world finally cottoned on to A SPACE, Jon Tashco goes and pisses off with all the talent. It was monstrous.

As far as I was concerned, personality, looks and all, Jon was a heel for doing that. Alice and I didn't agree on this, though. 'Come on, Sass, it's business. The artists didn't have to leave Stuart – no one was holding a gun to their heads.' Which was true, I guess. Still, it struck me as disloyal.

To give him credit, Jon had opened his gallery, Tashco, as far away from the hallowed portals of A SPACE as you could get, in Hoxton Square. It was doing really well, getting loads of press and attracting the American art collectors. Maybe Alice was right and I was being too precious, but something in me couldn't forgive Jon.

He'd asked me to come and join him the first month after he left. He'd even offered me a partnership, fifty-fifty, but out of a misguided sense of loyalty to Stuart, I'd stayed. Jon said he understood.

I didn't really have a choice. As fantastic an opportunity as Jon's offer was, I couldn't walk out on Stuart – not when he was in such a state. I couldn't bear seeing him like that. He was a total wreck. I'd rather be yelled at than watch him sinking the way he had.

He'd slunk around like a wounded dog, hardly saying a word for the first two months after Jon left. He lost loads of weight and started drinking. How do men do that? Lose weight while drinking? Even sticking to my recommended fourteen units of alcohol a week, I balloon.

The drinking was pretty serious for a while actually. One night in particular he got really maudlin and hung onto to me like I was a rock and he was a drowning man. 'You won't leave me, will you, Sassy?' he'd pleaded.

And looking into those crazed eyes, I'd decided that it was my responsibility to save him, to stand by him and help him pull A SPACE and himself back together.

Despite being part of the new immorality movement, I felt so sorry for him. I'd stroked his head and told him not to worry because I was in it for the long haul. 'We'll be OK, mate,' I'd reassured him. 'Anyway, who wants to go to Hackney for their art? Believe me, Stuart,' I'd said with a confidence I didn't feel, 'Tashco will be closed in a month.'

Famous last words.

When Tashco didn't close down but became a huge suc-cess, things with Stuart became immeasurably worse. The essentially decent, albeit tight-fisted guy I'd come to work for turned into the miserable paranoid git I now crept around to avoid.

There were no more tears or references to Jon, and any feeling I'd once had that I was part of a team effort were eradicated by Stuart's sniping and constant criticism. Our relationship had gone downhill. Instead of feeling like I was part of a team, it now seemed that there was a wall between us and I was on the side labelled, 'lackey'.

Three months ago in a fit of desperation I'd swallowed my sense of loyalty and rung Jon up. I told him I'd changed my mind about working for him, only to find he'd hired an American – Alice.

'I'm sorry, darling, but she's adorable. She's here with me now in fact, looking at your Flatmate Wanted ad,' he'd told me. 'Here, let me put her on. Sorry about the job, but Alice has got the best sense of humour I've come across since you,' he said, as if that should make me feel better. Funnily enough, once I met her it did.

It occurred to me then that Stuart had disappeared at the same time last week on a similarly mysterious appointment. Flicking through the diary pages, the plot thickened – there was no entry for last week either. I picked up the now warm can of V&T.

'Shit!' I screamed, spitting the contents all over the diary. Stuart, the bastard, had put his bloody cigarette out in my can.

Gross!

List of People who Erode my Self-esteem

1   All the men I have ever slept with.
2   My boss.
3   The ticket guys at Notting Hill station.
4   The red-headed woman who sneers when I refer to forties frocks as War Wear.
5   My bank manager, who rang me up last week and told me that maybe I should start thinking of a pension now that I'm getting on a bit! The cheek.
7   My mother.
8   My sister.

After I'd finished mopping up the appointment book, I tried to call Alice to tell her about my monumental failure with Stuart vis-à-vis the New York operation. I was seeing her tonight at the latest Tashco opening, and I knew it would be her first question. The answering machine was on at the gallery, though, so I called Sophie.

Besides girlfriendly sympathy and advice, gossip is the next best thing for building self-esteem. Sophie was v. much the girl to turn to for wicked gossip. She was a fashion editor at *Class*, a magazine pitched at a rarefied income bracket. So rare, in fact, that it was always pegged to go bust. She could always be relied on to have a scurrilous piece of scandal on hand.

If there was a downfall taking place in London's social echelons, Sophie was there – she would have seen the whole thing. She was always talking of selling her whereabouts to *News of the World*.

She was known around her circle of Sloaney friends as 'a hoot'. With looks like hers, trouble and men clung to her like mould to the stuff in our fridge. She had legs where other girls have necks. There has been a lot of talk around the tracks that some bits of her anatomy came from LA. When this idea was put to her, she just looked out from under her thick black fringe and laughed enigmatically.

Wherever the rest of her came from, her hair was all hers

– all three feet of it. Basically she's a long-haired brunette in a world of shoulder-length blondes. I'd met her when I was still at Goldsmith's. She'd been dating a bloke I'd been mooning over for months. It wasn't until she'd chewed him up and spat him out that he got round to fancying me, and by then I was more interested in Sophie.

We've basically been inseparable ever since, although she still gets first crack at any man I fancy, and usually I follow the tradition of losing interest in them as soon as she does. Sophie was my prototype for the new immorality.

After years of feeling invincibly young, we were now both living in constant fear of our impending thirtieth birthdays.

Sophie is the only truly liberated woman I know. She treats men like they treat women and means it. Men respect that she doesn't call and is never home whenever they do. Also, she is religiously late and never stays for breakfast – nor does she take them back to her place. 'A man on my sheets, I don't *think* so!' Like she says, sex is a messy business – let them clean it up.

Sometimes she has more than one bloke on the go, and sometimes I even find myself feeling sorry for them – not that I would ever let on to her, obviously.

She has this theory that men have been getting the best deal for, like, aeons, and now it's the girls' turn. 'Just for a generation or so,' she soothes the men who dare inspect the rationale behind her theory. 'Three generations tops – then we go for the equality thing! Fair enough?'

Today she was dishing on her boss – so what's new? Sophie is one of the few of my friends who understands what I *don't* see in Stuart – then again she never liked Jon Tashco either. For a Sloane, she's got a lot of worker solidarity attitude. It was she who gave me the strength to say no to Tashco when he came begging me to work for him. 'Sure, Saskia, you're going to work in the East End – like, *hello*?'

Anyway, today she was dishing on her boss, who's got some sort of minor title that doesn't give him an income but which he uses on his cheques anyway. He had been caught in flagrante (again) with Richard, the boy who does their odd jobs.

It seems to me that the upper classes risk a lot more for the sake of sex compared to the poor old middle class. I mean, my father was never even caught having sex with my mother, as far as I know.

'Are you coming to Tashco's opening tonight? Should be a good one, everyone's going to be there,' I asked hopefully. I was intending to drag her along to keep my mind off Jon and his new girlfriend.

'Yeah, right, everyone's *sooooo* interested in a bloke who travelled down his own T-cells with a laser camera,' she sneered.

'I take it that's a no?'

'That's a definite no. I think I'd rather strip my split ends than venture into the East End. You go and take the art world by storm for both of us.'

I wasn't sure I liked her attitude. 'Art world by storm' cracks are not really what I wanted to hear just when I was finally coming to terms with the reality that I was never going to take the art world by anything more than a light drizzle. It smarted that she could be so flippant about something which had once been so close to my heart – still, that was when I'd had a few too many drinks.

'A bit hard to take anything by storm in these boots, apart from a war zone,' I joked, not letting on how much her remark had hurt. 'My black satin shoes were marinated in Bloody Marys last night!'

'Oh, yes, the famous table-dancing gig,' she teased. 'Call me tomorrow, tell me how you go,' she said. Was the whole of London privy to my shame?

'Besides, I'm going to New York to do a big shoot for the

mag and I've got models and photographers coming out of my ears.'

'Brilliant image,' I said. 'So when are you going?'

'The day after our birthday, which is a bit of a drag as I was planning to party my way into the big Three-0.'

'I was thinking of going to New York with Alice,' I said, hoping that talking about it would make it happen. 'You know she's got a brownstone there. She half-owns with her brother Philip.'

'Brilliant! Can we use it?'

'Huh?'

'The house, where is it?'

'Fifth Avenue, I think. Why?'

'You're kidding! This is so fab – exactly what I need.'

Before I could ascertain exactly why it was that Alice's brownstone was so brilliant, the buzzer went.

'Look, Sophie, I've got to go, but we're still on for tomorrow at Albert's, aren't we?' I'd decided to forgive Albert now that I realised what a favour he'd done me by getting rid of Emmanuel. It was like he always said, 'Boyfriends come and go, but a hairdresser is for life.' Actually it was on his marketing brochure.

'Definitely. My hair needs a deep *penetrative* conditioning more than I do,' she joked.

We agreed to meet at four and I walked back out to the gallery kind of hopeful that a thief might have walked in and stolen the whole show. Fat chance.

It was Emmanuel who was standing in the middle of A SPACE. Tall, dark and drop-dead handsome – that's drop dead as in I wish he would, the smarmy, arrogant, no-good prig. This was the bloke I had danced on tables and polluted my liver and shoes to get over. What had I been thinking of?

I was left to wonder why I hadn't taken Sophe's more traditional remedy for getting over a man and stuck everything ever associated with him in a garbage bag and squirted bleach all over it. There was still a rather nice pair of D&G jeans of his in my bottom drawer, if I remembered correctly. I made a note to put that on my Must Do list for this evening. On second thoughts, they looked rather good on me.

He began to walk towards me, his arms outstretched as if I was a daughter he'd put into a work camp when I was a child. And now he wanted to make up. Unlikely.

I cursed my footwear, realising that these boots were going to allow him to tower over me. If I had been wearing my heels, at least I'd have had the satisfaction of looking down on him.

'Saskia,' he sighed, pulling me to him. 'You are looking, how do you say it, er, well. *Non?*'

Emmanuel is the type of Frenchman who has lived in London for, like, twelve years and yet he still says stuff like, 'How do you say it? I don't know the English word.'

Alice was right; I don't suppose that what I had with Emmanuel was ever anything as serious as love, but at twenty-nine it's a comfort to know you have an admirer – 'a swain or two hanging in the wings', as Sophie puts it. But now I was over him. I mean it, I really was. I had my career and my holiday to think of now. It was just a shame that the two were mutually exclusive.

He was looking around the gallery like he'd just been deposited by aliens. Emmanuel is really big on playing the hapless Frenchman abroad. He's always telling anyone who'll listen with a Gallic shrug of the shoulders that he can't understand the English. I don't think he likes us much either – and our food! *Merde!* For some reason, though, he's superglued himself to us as a freelance writer for a swag of French and Italian art mags.

I met a French ex-girlfriend of his when I first started dating him. She tried to warn me, God love her. 'Emmanuel is the worst kind of Frenchman,' she decreed. 'We wouldn't put up with such behaviour in a man in France. That's why he stays here,' she explained.

At the time I put her bitching down to sour grapes, but no doubt she had the inside info. There were probably 'Not Wanted' posters up all over Calais, warning customs officers to approach him with extreme disdain.

'Saskia?' he said, in the voice that reeked of 'Can it really be you?'

I told him that it really was me, as he suspected. Being a civilised woman of sound emotional disposition, I didn't clout him over the head with 'White Mood Swing' like he deserved. No, I calmly kissed him – but only on one cheek, which left him pecking at an empty space beside me. I do so love doing that. A girl's got to get her kicks where she can.

'Stuart has truly, how do you say – excelled himself this time,' he sneered, looking around the gallery. 'Can you believe he urged me to come and see this rubbish?'

I folded my arms and said that I could. That was what galleries did all the time, ask critics to come and see their shows, I reminded him.

'I wouldn't waste my ink on it,' he scoffed.

'Just your breath,' I shot back.

'Can we speak, Saskia?' he asked, in the stilted English of a foreign phrase-book reader.

'Well, I'm not having any trouble myself,' I told him.

'Oh, Saskia, always that prickly English humour of yours. But you are looking, so, so, what is the English word – *jolie*? Tell me, what have you done to yourself?'

Now that is a question I truly hate. It implies that I've finally taken a course of corrective action on my appearance that I should have taken years ago. I felt like saying 'got over you', but sarcasm is Stuart's department. I like to think I'm above that myself.

'Thanks,' I said. 'How kind of you to say so.'

'Don't be sad, Saskia, I beg of you. Don't get, how do you say in English, sour?'

'Bitter?' I suggested, narrowing my eyes.

'This is the word – bitter. I have come to say, how do you say it? Sorry.'

'Sorry?'

'Yes. I think to myself, poor little Saskia. I must tell her sorry for walking out. I got, how do you say it in English, cold feet? For me, Saskia, it was time to move on. I was scared to tell you. That is why now I want to be honest with you. It is not that I am not fond of you, *chérie*. You are, how do you say in English . . . a remarkable girl?'

'A remarkable girl, perchance?' I offered. My arms were still folded, which in body language means Fuck off, I'm not interested, take your poxy compliments elsewhere!

'The thing is,' he stuttered, not reading my body talk, 'I was afraid I must, how you say in English – break it up with you? Is this how you say it, end the affair? I ask my friend and he tells me the phrase is chuck you, and I say *non*, this is an ugly phrase. It is garbage that one chucks, not my Saskia.'

'How kind,' I said between gritted teeth.

But Emmanuel didn't bother grappling with my sarcasm. His arms were gesticulating wildly like Napoleon rousing the troops before Waterloo. There was no stopping this guy; he wasn't even pausing to breathe. 'I say to him that this is not what I wish to do – this "chuck you". My friend says the verb dump is also good, or otherwise drop. Can you understand this, *chérie*, without pain? Can you understand that I wish you to be dropped?'

'What?' I yelped, like a dog that's been hit about the head with a rolled-up newspaper. I couldn't believe this was actually happening to a liberated, bleach-squirting girl like me with plans for her career and a holiday in New York pencilled in for a few weeks' time.

I was being dumped/chucked/dropped?

Men and women have had an unspoken agreement for years. By not calling, by not turning up for a date and then not calling to apologise, a relationship becomes void. An official announcement on these occasions is considered a tad déclassé in most circles.

But if there was any dropping to be done, take it from me, girls prefer to act as 'the dropper' and it is the mark of the new age bloke who values his testicles, to allow a girl this small privilege by playing the role of 'the dropped'. This Gaelic bastard couldn't just prance in here and *dump* me – especially after I'd already danced on tables to get him out of my system!

Could he?

This was taking the new immorality thing a bit too bloody far. I mean, I know I tipped out a beggar's rag this morning, but hadn't I suffered enough? Wasn't it bad enough that my boss was gunning for me, that my V&T had fag ash in it and my best shoes were soaked in Bloody Mary? Although normally a robust girl with a background in hockey and a flexible take on gender roles, I was definitely not up for this. I had a reputation to think of. Of sorts.

I went over these salient points in my head while Emmanuel continued his soliloquy, sprinkling his linguistic stumblings with eloquent phrases like 'still be of mutual professional benefit' and 'respect for personal space'. 'I don't want you to take this chucking up, how do you say it? To be chucked, is this correct? I don't know this English word.'

'Nor do I,' I told him bluntly. I might have a low pride threshold when it comes to men, but even I draw the line at giving them the words to dump me.

He seemed a bit cross that I wasn't falling about in tears, so he tried to add a bit of drama by placing his hands on my shoulders and kissing my forehead.

This was excruciatingly annoying.

'Saskia, Saskia. Always the prickly pear. You must not feel bitter. It's not your fault I don't love you any more.' Still holding my shoulders, he shook me like one of those baby-killing childcare workers, and I wondered if he was close enough for me to bite off that sharp little nose I'd once so delighted in kissing.

'Ta for that,' I snarled, rolling my eyes for effect.

'I just want you to know that I still care for you. Even though the time has come for me to chuck you, I have not stopped caring for you.'

'Gee, thanks,' I told him, virtually all squirmed out.

Having run my tongue along the ridges of his torso only the night before last, I now felt an overwhelming sense of nausea, but maybe that was the cigarette butt going to work on my stomach lining.

'You have a lot to give, *chérie*. One day you will find the man who does not want to chuck you. You just have so much to give,' he reassured me.

'Oh, no. If you're thinking of borrowing money, Emmanuel, forget it.'

'Prickly, prickly Saskia,' he laughed, pinching my cheek. 'I mean it, *mon petit chou*, you are a very sexy girl, although if you don't mind me saying, your breasts need a little work. Don't be bitter, it's nothing personal, I don't want this to spoil our friendship.' He stroked my face and I felt a shiver go through me. 'I mean it, Saskia. I don't want to see you get hurt.'

'Hurt? You think you're capable of hurting me?' I let out a hard, brittle laugh.

'I'm not blind, you know. I know what's going on here with Stuart.'

Stuart? Did he actually say Stuart? Surely he wasn't suggesting I was sleeping with Stuart? 'Have I missed something?' I asked. 'Nothing is going on with Stuart.'

'Saskia, Saskia,' he sighed, still leaning on my shoulders.

My arms were still tightly folded like a barrier. 'My little ingénue. You think everything is a garden of Eden, full of people who care deeply for art.'

'Well, hardly that,' I told him, thinking about *Experiences in White*, and wondering how I was going to make anyone feel deeply enough about them actually to part with money.

'People can get hurt, Saskia. Even little girls like you.'

'Don't patronise me,' I warned him.

He looked at me meaningfully, as if he was waiting for a camera to zoom in for a close-up on him.

'Take a warning from a friend. Stay out of this business.'

'Listen, I don't know what you're talking about but I've heard enough. Take your warnings, your insinuations and your "prickly" shit and get out. You and I are never going to be friends. I want you out of this gallery now.'

He raised his eyebrows and smiled.

'Now!' I roared.

'Sure, you want me to leave, I'll leave. I was afraid that you would take this chucking-off badly. My friend warned me of this.'

'Look, mate, you chucking me isn't what's upset me. Besides, you didn't dump me, I dumped you, chucked you, dropped you, broke it off, severed the connection. I danced on tables last night with sheer exuberance that I was finally shot of you. And get this, you were only ever a sympathy fuck.' I could see I'd stung him. Not that he'd stopped grinning for a minute, but the grin was looking a bit frozen. A bit stiff. I was getting the boot in and loving it. This was much more rewarding than squirting bleach on his jeans.

'Yes, a sympathy fuck and a lousy one at that, and if I'm ever really desperate, which I never will be, obviously, I'd never consent to no-strings sex with you. Do you understand that. I chucked you. *Comprends*? If not, I'll email you the relevant bits.'

To my horror he embraced me again.

'Ah, yes, I heard about the dancing. But this is why I came. I don't want to think of you like this, making, how you say, a fool for yourself?'

At this point I was just standing there with my mouth open in shock/humiliation/embarrassment/outrage – take your pick. This guy's ego was incorrigible.

Suddenly Emmanuel was pulling me to him. Wrenching my chin roughly towards his mouth, he pressed his tongue down my throat in what I can only describe as the most revolting kiss I have ever endured. PS: He'd had pesto sauce for lunch.

I spluttered, struggled and then choked on his tongue but I refused to give up. For a minute there I thought he must be after Stuart's cigarette butt.

When I finally managed to pull away, he chucked me under the chin like I was his kid sister. 'I'm serious about Stuart though,' he said as he turned to leave. 'Be careful. Watch out for yourself. I'll come by to pick up my jeans on the weekend, hey?' he added. Unfortunately he'd walked off before I'd had time to detail my bleaching plans for said trousers and other sundry items he may have left within my reach.

Survival in the City list

1 Don't make eye contact on the tube.
2 Don't panic when the train is stuck in a tunnel and someone starts feeling your breasts.
3 Always carry something that can be used as a weapon in an emergency.
4 Cultivate poise, esp in department stores, and don't try to unlock cabinets by self.
5 Carry money in your bra – so as to avoid losing it to muggers, and to pad bra out.
6 Be prepared to fight men in suits for cabs, especially in the City where boys like to play rough.
7 Familiarise yourself weekly with all vulnerable points on a man's body (see 6 and 1 above).
8 Avoid the Northern line where possible.
9 Do not allow longings for love/success, etc. to overwhelm you in inappropriate situations.
10 Say 'I already have that copy' to *Big Issue* sellers.

Emmanuel was dashing down the street as the unfamiliar American voice started up. The acoustics of this place were designed for close-range cultured whispering – there was an echo that made the voice rumble. The voice seemed to be coming from every corner of the gallery, like the voice of God booming down from Mount Sinai or something.

'I'm sorry, I didn't realise you were busy. I should have left.'

I spun around, scanning the corners of *Experiences in White* for my interlocutor. The disembodied voice was deep and totally unrecognisable.

This must have been how Moses felt, only I was far too flustered and cross to deal with sacred covenants at this particular moment. I gave whoever it was a clue to my mood by folding my arms across my chest and furrowing my brow. Then I waited for them to reveal themselves.

'Have I come at a bad time?' the voice asked.

Well, that was an understatement and I didn't bother to respond. I tapped my foot for quite some time before the man in question eventually gave himself up.

Walking calmly out of one of the antechambers where we sometimes exhibited sculptures, I eyed him up and I eyed him down and then, seeing what a god he was, I eyed him down again. My knees wobbled involuntarily. He was everything I've always wanted in a man and then some.

He was smiling, and something knowing within me told me that I was the cause of his mirth. I began to redden.

'I've startled you, haven't I? Should I come back later?' he asked, grinning superciliously.

He was tall and very, very handsome, the sort of handsome that makes you catch your breath and realise you look nothing like Meg Ryan or Kate Winslet or anyone slim and nice like that. Due to my hangover, I hadn't spent enough time on my appearance that day – well, none at all to be perfectly honest!

The only effort I'd made to look good was to pull a lipstick across my lips. But as I stood there under the scrutiny of this Adonis, I began to fear that even the lipstick may have been one of those nasty dated colours like off-purple.

It must have been, because he was staring at my mouth v. oddly. I began to curse myself for not buying one of those ultra-beige shades recommended to me by an assistant last week during one of my after-work dashes around the Selfridges cosmetics section.

'Beige suits you,' the blindingly beautiful girl at Lancôme had promised me disinterestedly. 'I bet you say that to all the girls,' I'd told her. Now I wish I hadn't been so sassy. I should have humbly accepted her words of advice and debited my Selfridges Gold Card another twenty quid. 'Fuck it!' I said under my breath.

'What?' said my stranger, who, in contrast to me, had spared no effort in presenting himself as God's gift to womankind. He was superb. Wearing a pinstriped, tailor-made suit that perfectly complemented the delectable contours of his body, he exuded Platinum Card-ness, power and a double helping of toe-curling sex appeal. He also had rather nice eyes, I noticed dreamily, before I went back to my natural state of self-loathing.

'Nothing, I was just muttering under my breath,' I told him breezily. God, I was hopeless with men like this. Give me a weedy artist in a pair of paint-splattered 501s and I'm all wit and one-liners. But faced with a man I might actually want to bed, and this is how I react. I may as well start dribbling and get the whole ordeal over with, I thought to myself.

Standing there in my bedraggled white cheesecloth, freshly creased by my tussle with the security men, and my Israeli army boots, I could just imagine what he was thinking. I mean, this was definitely a guy used to sexy little Chanel suits or Armani slacks, I could just tell.

To be fair, it was like the first time I'd ever worn these boots to work, combat gear being seriously frowned upon by Stuart and the Bond Street area at large basically. I'd love to admit to being the Imelda Marcos of Notting Hill, but apart from my vintage orange hessians, my only other pair of high-heeled shoes was soaked in Bloody Mary.

As he came closer, I noticed that his eyes crinkled up at the corners like he'd spent a lifetime chuckling at a good joke. I hated him for catching me in the sloppy embrace with Emmanuel. And more to the point, I was wondering how many of those 'prickly pears' and ''Mon petit chou' he might have heard. God, what must he have witnessed?

Most troubling of all was an overwhelming fear that my lipstick, whatever colour it was, may not have stayed on my lips as the marketing blurb promised it would. I'd been let down before by smudge-proof mascara and non-shine foundation. Perhaps kiss-proof lipstick was about to be the latest disappointment in my cosmetics bag?

But like the mature, career-oriented girl I was about to become, I put my worries aside, and, with an eye to my commission, I went into professional mode. I could smell the cash on this guy and I could smell a need within him to spend it.

Never mind that *Experiences in White* were crap, we had a massive stockroom. That was it: I could take him downstairs and ravish him. Who knows – maybe he'd buy something and Stuart would tell me I deserved a holiday and suggest that when I return, I take over all curatorial responsibilities. This could be my big break.

'Hello? Are you OK?' he asked, waving his hands before my eyes.

'Sorry,' I murmured, coming to. 'I was lost in thought. I was just surprised – I didn't hear you come in. I'm Saskia Williams, by the way,' I simpered, extending my hand.

To my horror, instead of the firm handshake I'd been anticipating, the madman took my hand to his lips and kissed it.

I snatched it back as if it had been bitten. 'Excuse me, I can't imagine what you must think of me,' I babbled incoherently. 'Let me get you a drink. Coffee, tea, wine, vodka and tonic?

'Vodka and tonic sounds perfect,' he drawled.

'Oh dear, you see, well, actually, we don't really have vodka and tonic. Not in the true sense of the term. Well, we do, but it's got a cigarette butt in it, I'm afraid. Shut up, Saskia.'

He smiled. 'Wine sounds perfect, then.'

I blushed. 'Chardonnay all right?'

'Excellent.'

'Right then,' I said, gazing into his eyes. Basically I was glued to the spot, like an installation we had in the gallery once of a wax bloke in a suit holding a hundred-dollar bill. Highly ironic – at least, according to the Dutch museum who purchased it for twelve grand.

I tried to look ironic as I took in the glory that was this man's physique. Apart from the odd Jeff Koons type, the art world is sadly bereft of hunky guys. It's a problem with the artistic lifestyle I guess – late nights, poor diet, too much turpentine and not nearly enough time spent down the gym. Well any to be perfectly frank.

This man, on the other hand, was really quite delicious.

I doubt if he'd ever come face to face with formaldehyde fumes, let alone splashed it over his suit. His dark hair had a few grey strands in it and although recently cut – no doubt at Trumpers – it was still long enough for a Leonardo DiCaprio flick. If he'd flicked it at that very moment, though, I would have wet myself, such was the precarious state of my libido post-snog with Emmanuel.

'Sorry, what did you say your name was?' I asked.

He raised one eyebrow.

'Your name?' I repeated.

He grinned some more. I read somewhere once that if you smile without blinking seven times in a minute, people perceive you as dangerous. His lids remained firmly still, the seconds ticked on. Not so much as a flicker. His teeth were white, perfectly aligned and could only have come from America – unsurprising really as so did his accent.

'Sorry,' he chuckled. 'I shouldn't keep laughing at you, I'm being terribly selfish. Here, let me help.' He reached for the handkerchief in his top pocket. 'You have a little lipstick on your chin.'

Never have four words struck such horror into the heart of womankind as 'lipstick on your chin'. Talk about a death by humiliation. I certainly didn't need the added indignity of being dabbed with a stranger's handkerchief, that was for sure.

After I'd pelted downstairs to the loo in the storeroom, I was able to witness the full glory of my shame in the mirror.

A little lipstick on your chin had to be the euphemism of the century – knocking Captain Oates of the Antarctic's claim that he 'may be some time' right out of the water.

Far from living up to its no-smudge claim, the lipstick was everywhere. I looked like one of those kids on Kleenex commercials who has got stuck into Mummy' make-up. And that wasn't all. The tortoiseshell clip I'd put my hair up with this morning in an effort to make up for the fact that I couldn't find my brush, must have got caught up in Emmanuel's watch or something. It was now mounted at a skew-whiff angle on top of my head like a mock crown on top of a bird's nest. My hair, like my life, was a disaster of tangles and knots.

I pulled and tugged at the split-ended mess that was my over-bleached hair until I finally beat it into a surly submission. This was the limit: tomorrow I would teach my hair a lesson and have Albert cut it all off, and if he made a fuss I would threaten to sue him over the list business.

I wiped the offending lipstick off my chin and upper lip and gargled heartily. By the time I walked back into the gallery bearing his glass of cheap, room-temperature Chardonnay, I was even starting to get a little bit more of my charm and confidence back.

'Feeling better?' he asked kindly, accepting his glass.

'Thank you. I'm sorry, I didn't get your name,' I said smoothly, trying to leave my past fool-of-the-month guise behind me.

'That's right, I didn't get round to giving it to you, did I?' His eyes glinted with mischief. 'You must give me a price list before we go any further, and tell me, is that one over towards the door still available? "White Mood Swing", I think it's called. I particularly like the sense of irony the artist has captured there.'

'Are you insane?' I shrieked before I could stop myself. I'm going to have to break that habit before I hit thirty. Men have told me they find it a huge turn-off, especially when I do it after they've orgasmed and I haven't – as in, Hello? Are we finished here? I don't think so!

My toes stopped curling. Hang ten for a minute, I told them. Could I honestly fancy a bloke who appreciated anything about a painting entitled 'White Mood Swing'? Er, er, I hate to say it, but yes – probably. Libido is such a fickle mistress.

Ever the professional, I didn't roll on my back and howl with mirth, but clunk, clunked over to get my mystery man the list. 'Familiar with Jeff Hewit's work, Mr—?'

'No, but I'm starting off a small collection of British art. I'm after a good investment and these paintings by Jeff caught my eye as I was walking by. I spoke to Mr Dumass about his work on the phone, and he filled me in on this Hewit's CV. Sounds impressive enough. He tells me his paintings sold for around twenty thousand at the last show. I should tell you that I'm looking for a safe investment,' he added.

I looked at him sympathetically, trying to convince myself how it was possible to still fancy a guy exhibiting such toxic taste.

'I can see by the way you're looking at me that I've outed myself as a philistine. Does linking investment to art appal you, Miss Williams?'

Let's get this much clear, I wanted to say. Just the fact that you fancy *Experiences in White* at all appals me. I'm not so averse to minimalism that I don't love a white wall or crisp white linen or even a clear dressing table on a good day, but these unprimed canvases which the artist described as 'a tongue-in-cheek discussion on emotions', were exploring new realms of crap.

Jon always said that when an artist uses the words 'tongue' and 'cheek' in the same sentence, it's time to stick the old index finger down the throat. That said, I wasn't so appalled that I wasn't doing a bit of mental arithmetic to work out the potential commission I could expect. These paintings were not cheap, whatever else they were.

I shuffled papers purposefully, acutely aware of his eyes boring into me from behind. Jeff Hewit's CV was proof of the old adage, It's not what you know but how much your friends earn. In a nutshell, the reason his work sold for so much at his last show was that his sycophantic relatives and friends bought them all at madly inflated prices. Aristocrats like sticking together even more than artists do. As far as I knew, he'd never sold any of his paintings on the open market.

My skin was prickling with the intensity of knowing that this stranger, whatever his name was, was behind me, staring unblinkingly into my spine. I located the offending price sheet and turned around to find him six inches from me rather than the six feet I was counting on. Instead of letting out a startled yelp, however, I found myself exhaling dreamily as the sedative effect of his hypnotic scent took hold.

'Miss Williams!'

'Please, call me Saskia,' I stuttered meaninglessly. 'I'm sorry, I still didn't catch your name.' I passed him the list and almost swayed, drugged with my own pheromones.

He glanced over the sheet and I noticed that he held back a wince as he took a sip of the disgusting wine Stuart had taken to serving patrons since Jon had left. He muttered something about the time and looked distractedly at his watch.

'Yes, that seems to be in order. You've convinced me, Saskia, I'll take the whole show.'

'You'll what?' I squeaked.

'I'll send my man around tomorrow morning to finalise payment.'

As I looked around the gallery at the blank canvases, it dawned on me: the full enormity of both this guy's bad taste and the hitherto undreamed-of benefits of the big commission I'd just earned. I could already afford my fare to New York – on Concorde if I fancied.

'Oh, and thank you for the wine, most refreshing,' he added without a trace of sarcasm. He passed me his business card and his still full glass of antifreeze and left.

Life Skills I have Yet to Acquire

1   How to get CDs in and out of the case without breaking the case.
2   How to keep my clothes rack from falling down.
3   How to eat in bed without dropping crumbs.
4   How to froth milk in espresso machine without scalding arm.
5   How to have adult interactions with my mother without regressing to infantile faces.
6   How to stop cab drivers talking to me without making them hate me and take slow route.
7   How to keep my desires and needs from lunging out of me in inappropriate situations
8   How to stop buying clothes two or more sizes too small in the hope that one day I'll lose weight.
9   How to lose weight.
10 How to keep my bras from getting tangled up with my stockings and tights and my underwear drawer as a whole from turning into a big ball.

Arriving at the Tashco opening, the first thing I noticed was that Alice had dyed her hair. It was now an alarming shade of fire-engine red, hard not to notice. She said she felt like a change at lunch, and that Jon had helped her do it in the sink of the gallery's basement loo. I envied her seize-the-day-approach, only I wasn't too sure about her choice of colour.

'What do you think?' she asked, doing a spin.

I was her friend, so I was more or less obliged to lie. I said that it looked great but in a non-committal, we-both-know-I'm-lying voice.

'Liar, liar, pants on fire, Saskia Williams,' she laughed. 'Don't panic, it's just the wash-out stuff. I wanted to give Jim a fright because he's always going on about me being a blonde bimbo. I thought I'd teach him a lesson.'

'Oh?' I said. 'OK. So what lesson might that be, exactly?' I enquired.

'Whatever,' she laughed. 'My image needed shaking up anyway.' She put her arm around me. 'Come on, let's get some Becks.'

Trying not to stare, I agreed that Becks was the very best plan we could have hatched and followed her through the art crowd, by now spewing out of the gallery and onto Hoxton Square itself. Tashco was a hot ticket. I even spotted a television crew interviewing someone who looked liked one of the It girls who had a column in *The Times*.

Observers had been wondering for the last few years about the reason for London's vibrant art scene. The answer was obvious to the cognoscenti – free beer. In this instance the sponsors, Becks, hadn't even attempted to set up a stand but were doling it out from crates on the back of a truck. It was an art mosh-pit.

It was fortunate that my dress was of the pre-crushed variety, I decided as we pushed our way through the crowd – not that I was grumbling, though, the art crush opening is the sacred bastion of the art world. Recently Stuart had suggested not having any more openings at A SPACE, decreeing them a waste of money. But even he knew that was taking economy a bit far.

'I mean, talk about a travesty,' Alice had said when I told her. 'Openings *are* the art world. Take away the booze and there *is* no *world*. Just art objects displayed in a space.'

She was right. The art world was a kind of Narnia, and the door through which we entered was the art bash. All around us wannabe artists vied with suits and art world grandees for beer, space and a sound bite. Alice and I found a semi-quiet spot on the steps of the Blue Note, ostensibly to discuss my future as a curator. As if!

'Dish, girl,' she said.

And dish I did.

'*The* Piers Dexter?' she screamed, as if my ear was on the other side of Hoxton Square, as opposed to the millimetre from her mouth that it was.

'I swear,' I said, when my eardrum had stopped vibrating.

'*The* Piers Dexter – you're not mobbing me up, are you?'

'Why, is he someone I should have heard of?' I enquired, nonchalance personified as a bunch of girls in paint-splattered overalls pushed past, excoriating my face with their satchels in the process.

'You can't be serious?' she repeated like a stuck record.

I wanted to say, 'No, you're right, I was just making the

whole thing up for your diversion,' but instead I raised my eyebrows a fraction and waited for her wide-eyed wonderment to die down.

I can do mature, you know. I examined my nails as if Piers and his fame meant nothing to a sophisticated seen-it-all girl-of-the-world like me. My ego had been waiting for an opportunity like this all day, a chance to look cool and in control.

'But you must have heard of Piers Dexter,' she insisted. 'He only owns half of America. He practically invented the word *web*.' She grabbed my wrist and squeezed as hard as she could, trying to transfer her excitement into my system by osmosis.

I stuck to my guns of nonchalance. 'Web? Who is this guy, Spider Man?'

'As in www?' she explained, looking at me as if I'd blown a chip.

'Oh yeah, that web,' I mumbled, my ego starting to contract. Shit, I had to get out more, out there in cyberspace where it was clearly all happening. Even Sophie surfed the web now, and Sophie never went anywhere that hadn't been deemed hallowed ground generations ago. She still hadn't been as far east as Hoxton Square.

'Seriously, this man's got more millions than I've got shoes,' she told me, holding up one of her own stiletto-clad feet for emphasis.

I nodded solemnly. This meant a great many millions indeed. Alice has more shoes than I've had failed relationships. While I find it hard to keep three pairs on the road at any one time, she probably keeps Vivienne Westwood solvent.

A conservative estimate of her shoe wealth would put it up there with a small Latin American country's national debt. Vivienne Westwood's shoemakers could see her coming. Well who couldn't? Ten-inch platforms tend to make a girl a bit conspicuous.

'All right, so he's rich, but his taste in art sucks,' I rationalised, holding my nails up to the light as if I was hardly following the conversation. I really must stop biting them, I decided. Yes: I'd add that to my list of Life Skills I have yet to Acquire.

Alice shook her head. 'Honey, I can forgive a man like Piers a lot. A hell of a lot.'

'He is kind of cute,' I conceded, thinking dreamily of his long, muscular body and the way he'd kissed my hand. For anyone else, an act like that would be schmaltzy. Well, all right, so it *was* schmaltzy, but it was stylishly schmaltzy! Besides, I didn't think I'd ever been close enough to fancy someone so rich before.

'*Kind* of cute?' she squealed. 'Are you dead, girlfriend?' A number of people in the square turned round to check us out. Death was still v. cool in the art world. 'There are women who'd give up their womb to bed Piers Dexter,' she pointed out. 'He might have the integrity of a shark, but when it comes with eyes like those, who gives a damn? Talk about carnivorous, though; that guy's truly deadly. There isn't an unmarried woman under thirty living in Manhattan who's heart he hasn't masticated and spat out.'

I felt slighted by this reference to under-thirties. Like I said, it's such a benchmark age. The subtext reading, Piers Dexter doesn't bother masticating women *over* thirty! Alice was immune to such subtlety herself, being a safe bet at twenty-four.

'Oh, I don't know,' I sighed, casting my gaze around the flotsam and jetsam of the London art world, who, gathered in their motley tribal groupings, looked suddenly unappealing. Sucking on bottles of Becks, dragging on Marlboro Lights, trying to find someone important enough to speak to who might be drunk enough to deign to speak to them. I tried to envisage Piers Dexter among them but failed.

'He's not bad, but I wouldn't miss *Frasier* to sleep with him,' I told her.

'Yeah, right,' she said, in a tone that implied she doubted my sincerity.

I was starting to feel exposed, sitting there discussing a man I'd spent all afternoon fantasising about. It was as if he was no more than an object; what's more, an object at the centre of a billion other women's fantasies, if Alice's theory was right. This concept sort of clashed with my sense of individuality, fancying a man with such mass appeal.

Normally I go for blokes that other women wouldn't touch with a bargepole. Men like Emmanuel, who I spotted on the other side of the square flirting ten to the dozen with a dishy blonde artist recently bought by the Tate. My mother's always warning me not to spoil my chances by aiming too high.

'Ladies, how's tricks?' Jim's distinctive voice interrupted. Standing on the step in front of us, he threw an arm over each of our shoulders and pressed our faces to his groin. Subtle, like. That's Jim.

'The beautiful Sophia not with you tonight?' he asked.

'Aren't we good enough for you, then?' Alice laughed good-naturedly as I fought to free my face. Jim is about as far from my sexual phenotype as it is possible to get and still be within the human species. I couldn't see what Alice saw in him.

'I thought for a minute you weren't coming,' Alice pouted, by which time he had encased her face in his hands and was snogging her noisily.

Jim was the weak link in my respect for Alice. With an IQ that could entertain a cocktail party of Stephen Hawking wannabes, she was mentally challenged when it came to men like Jim. Public-school accent, poverty-stricken bank account and always with an eye to his next lay.

It caused me a great degree of chagrin that I had introduced her to Jim, and given the way she'd fallen for him, I felt a bit like someone who'd offered a cancer victim their first fag.

I waited for Jim's reaction to Alice's hair, which I was beginning to think suited her. With a bit of luck he'd hate it and they'd have an argument.

Jim is an artist, which basically precludes desirability on any count as far as I'm concerned. If you are the sort of girl who finds men irresponsible and chaotic, artists are your worst fears personified. Take it from me, you haven't smelt bad socks until you've bedded an artist.

Jim was the worst sort of artist – the sort that wants a show at the gallery where I work. Up until Tashco opened, that is. Before that he had followed me around like the bad smell that he is, but with the opening of Tashco he had diverted his attentions to Alice. A far more receptive focus, granted. I would have felt slighted if I wasn't so disgusted by him. Hairy hands have never been my style.

'God, you're looking good, babe,' he said, looking deeply into her eyes like he meant it.

'Babe?' I asked. 'You let him call you babe? What are you, a farm animal?'

But neither Alice nor Jim seemed to be listening. He was running his hands through her hair, although he still hadn't mentioned her change of colour. Was he just playing cool, or had he actually failed to notice the alarming red, I wondered?

'What's the show like?' he asked. 'I couldn't get in it was so packed. Fucking big crowd, huh? Jon must be celebrating.'

'Fantastic, have you met the artist?' Alice asked, in a cutesy sort of voice she never uses when she's with me.

'Give me a chance, I haven't even got a beer yet. I came looking for you straight away.'

God, he was smooth.

'Isn't he sweet,' Alice cooed, and I nodded.

The suspense was killing me. I had to know if Jim had clocked her hair. 'What do you think of Alice's hair?' I asked.

'It's lovely, isn't it? Lovely hair,' but he wasn't really paying it any attention; he was looking around the crowd for someone more interesting to talk to.

'Come with me,' Alice said, taking his hand. 'You don't mind, do you, Sass? I'll just take Jim in to see the work – we won't be a minute.' She winked and was leading him off before I'd had a chance to answer.

I would probably have got all maudlin about being left alone given the way my ego had been so bruised by Emmanuel, but just then Jon turned up and got me in one of his bear-hugs.

'Sassy! God, it's good to see you. A speck of sanity on my horizon. This evening has been mad, mad, mad. Talk about manic, I haven't stopped all day. *Vogue*'s been in – they're doing a big feature on the gallery.'

'Gee, that's great,' I said, enjoying the feel of his body against mine.

'And just now I've been giving an interview to Emmanuel for *Flash Art*. You're kind of seeing him, aren't you?' he asked, pulling away from me.

'What?' I asked, noticing his expectant look. All I could think about was whether he really fancied me, and if he did, why he never did anything about it – well, nothing definite. He was rubbing the side of my arm and when I took my time answering, he pinched me.

'Ow!' I yelled, pinching him back.

'Emmanuel, you were seeing him, weren't you?'

'Yeah, *was* seeing. I've dumped him now.' OK, so slight bending of facts, but I think Emmanuel owed me that much.

'About time too. I wondered when you were going to wake up. You're too good for a prat like him,' he said, giving my arm an affectionate squeeze. A shiver ran through me.

'My mother thinks I aim too high,' I told him, looking into his eyes. 'Actually even she might think that Emmanuel was beyond the pale, French etc.'

He laughed. 'It's the etceteras that have me worried,' he said staring straight back into my own eyes. If I didn't know better I would have said he was flirting. Get a grip, I told myself. Jon and I have always flirted, that's what platonic friendship with a single hetero man is all about, flirting. Doesn't mean anything. Course not.

'Anyway, *Flash Art* and *Frieze* are both going to profile the gallery in their next issue, apparently. I'm glad you came. I was so worried you wouldn't. I told Alice to lean on you.'

'You didn't have to do that. I would have come anyway,' I told him, inwardly whooping it up that he seemed so pleased to see me. He was wearing a black shirt, and a tie I had bought at Ozwald Boateng for his last birthday. I stroked it affectionately.

'My lucky tie,' he grinned, grabbing my hand. 'Have you had a chance to beat a path through to the show yet?'

'Not yet,' I admitted. 'I tried to get Sophie to come but she had to split her ends.'

'Sure,' he said, looking around at the crowd as if I bored him. He'd never really gone for Sophie, declaring her a 'mad Sloane with no sense of art', as if there was a division of Sloanes out there that were really sensible and the first to fall on the blade of the cutting edge.

I was almost tempted to repeat her scathing condemnation of Matt's work, but pulled myself back just in time. Why did I always feel like bitching him up these days? I mean, apart from the fact that he had ruined my boss's life and, *ipso facto*, mine? I couldn't help feeling slightly awkward around him now, seeing him in the gallery he'd set up without me. Seeing him successful, and, worse still, possibly with another girl.

I couldn't help wishing that things had never changed; that he was still with Stuart and me, drinking vodka martinis, being outrageous and rude about Hewit's *Experiences in White*. I felt a bit like the estranged wife who's been left with the difficult child, while her husband's gone off to pursue his own glamorous life with a new mistress.

'Looks like a good crowd,' I offered lamely.

Jon's face lit up. 'I knew you'd say that. He's brilliant, isn't he, totally fresh and the work's so vivid. I'm not joking, Saskia, this is a really exciting show,' he assured me. 'I know it's getting to be a tired theme, artists exploring their own anatomies and all, but with his grasp of new technology he'll blow everyone else out of the water. He's good, Sassy, really fucking hot.'

'Great! I mean, how nice. I mean, well, I knew you wouldn't show crap,' I stuttered. I could hardly say the same about A SPACE.

'I really think people are excited by his work, really responding well. I've already sold the installation on the invite to the Tate.'

'Great,' I enthused, gazing into his eyes for signs of deeper feelings.

'How's it going with Stuart?' he asked, suddenly serious.

'Yeah, well. Stuart's Stuart,' I muttered.

'Sorry, what did you say? I missed that.'

'I was just saying that, well, Stuart is Stuart,' I repeated, not knowing what the hell I was talking about. I couldn't concentrate and I inwardly cursed Alice for making me so self-conscious about a man I'd always felt so easy around.

Suddenly Jon was taking the clip from my hair and sweeping a stray lock back into place. It was as if his touch had ignited a flame in my head. I felt a blush shoot from my neck to my face.

It was the sort of familiar gesture that friends think nothing of, I told myself; I was reading far too much into everything. It was all part of turning thirty, I told myself. My longings for love were lunging out of me again, that was all. My need for reassurance of my desirability was making me misread perfectly innocent situations.

I smiled carefully. It was like old times after all.

Jon lowered his voice and looked earnestly into my face. 'Is he calming down a bit?' he asked.

'Who, Stuart. God, yeah, great. We've got a very exciting show up at the moment actually,' I lied. 'American collector walked in today and bought the lot. Really big, bold canvases,' I breezed, putting my hand to my nose to check it wasn't growing.

'Hewit, isn't it?'

Bloody hell – he'd sprung me. 'Er, yes, I mean, not as exciting as this show, obviously, but a good investment.' Shit. I tried pulling my head down into my neck.

Tashco looked at me with pity. 'You know, Saskia, I know why you stayed with Stuart and all, and I admire you, I really do, but promise me you'll be careful, OK?'

'Sure,' I nodded. 'But careful of what?'

He was about to say something when one of the art groupies, a gorgeous leggy blonde, interrupted us with a gushy pronouncement of the show's worth. 'Tashco dah-ling, it's fab. I can't believe you keep coming up with these discoveries!' She was heavily made-up and very, very influential and hip at the moment.

Jon needed to give face to this woman, and as a friend I should have had the grace to step aside and let him get on with it. But I didn't.

'Hardly that,' I sniped. 'We showed Matt at A SPACE last year.'

I hated myself as soon as I'd said it.

Jon looked at me as if I'd struck him. I could feel my

cheeks burning. I couldn't believe something so bitchy had come from my mouth and it wasn't even true, well, not strictly. Matthew was Tashco's last find while he was with Stuart, and Stuart hadn't wanted to show him, deeming him too 'edgy'. Thankfully I was saved from the dressing down I no doubt deserved because a bloke carrying far more Becks than he could manage dropped his load, spraying the leggy blonde with beer.

I left Tashco rubbing her legs down with his handkerchief and fought my way through the crowds spilling onto the street, in search of Alice. It was like finding a needle in a haystack. How hard can it be, finding a redhead tottering about in ten-inch heels in a sea of Doc Marten's?

The proverbial 'everyone' was here tonight. Gavin Turk sans baby, Link Leisure looking simply seventies, and there was a rumour that Damien Hirst was coming later with a crowd of pop stars.

Eventually I made out Jim's bald head from a sea of bald heads. One of the more useful things we learnt at art school was how to tell bald heads apart even with a blood alcohol level of ten and over. Very useful, as anyone at a London art opening will vouch. He was at the beer truck, asking for some more Becks. One of the blokes standing on the open-topped vehicle doling it out from the crates was having some sport with him.

'Go on then, you had one earlier, make me laugh or you're not getting another one,' he taunted.

Jim blushed all over his shaved scalp and then mumbled something I couldn't hear into the ear of his tormentor.

'Nah, boring, heard it before,' shouted the Becks guy loudly for the benefit of the crowd at large. 'Piss off! Next.'

'Three,' I said as Jim disappeared back into the crowd, red with embarrassment.

'G'day, Sass, what brings you all the way over here?' he asked. Baz had been distributing the beer at openings around

London for years. He was an Australian with striking looks and a big mouth, and wore those woven wristbands you get in Greece all over his arms.

When I'd first met him, he'd been really shy and wide-eyed. That's the art world, bound to make you twisted and cynical in the end, even if you are only on the periphery.

'Not love – or money, anyway,' I told him.

'Good crowd, eh? Your boss hasn't had this kind of turnout for a while.'

'I'll tell him you noticed.'

'Shit no, don't do that, he's hard enough to deal with as it is, Wanker that he is. Don't tell him I said that, neither!'

'Hurry up, chuck us a beer, will you,' an impatient voice called out behind me.

'You again? Make me laugh or you're not getting any,' he taunted, passing me my beers and winking.

I went over to where I'd seen Alice just before she fell off her platforms. Miraculously, Jim was helping her up.

'Thanks Sass,' he said as I passed him his beer. 'You should have got me to get them, I was just about to go over.'

I decided not to mention that I'd witnessed his humiliation with the beer bloke earlier. I sort of felt sorry for him. I guess blokes like Jim must get impervious to rejections, but just the same, it can't be a barrel of fun being an artist with no discernible future.

The canvas and the paint and the chance to create are one thing, but the egos, the arse-licking and the hypocrisy inherent in the art world are hell. Someone once said that you can be part of the art world or part of the real world, but no one has the ego for both. Actually I think it was Jon.

The rest of the opening was a blur. Alice finally dragged me in through the crowds to see the show, where there was a bloke taking polaroids of everyone's expression as they observed the wall-size video installation.

I have to admit that my expression was rapt. It was nothing

short of impressive, shooting down a T-cell. As close as I'd come to excitement all year, unless you count last month when I split my fifties pencil skirt falling down the marble steps of Versace on Bond Street. Sophie had dragged me along with her on one of her designer store romps, and as I tumbled down I remember seeing my whole life flash before my eyes in a kaleidoscope of multicoloured frocks.

Thank God the skirt had been leather (a find – a fiver at Portobello) or I would have slid the whole way down and possibly not even lived to tell the tale. No one said fashion was going to be an easy altar to worship at, Sophie had remarked after the security guard had scooped me up. Which was rich, given that she was the devotee.

As well as the video installation, there was a series of morphed images of cell structures and a translucent fibreglass cast of the artist. There was no denying that this artist was compelling. It made A SPACE seem so lame.

Crushed against a pillar, another more serious-looking girl was taking covert paparazzi shots of people she thought might matter. Everyone was hissing that Damien Hirst had been and gone with Jarvis Cocker, and that David Bowie was rumoured to be coming later. Practically everyone had sighted Brian Eno and a really nice lesbian couple related how they had been driven around in Madonna's limo when she'd been in London years ago. Everyone seemed to have a star story.

By nine o'clock people started to move on. Anyone that mattered had gone off to Groucho's, unless they had an invite to the party at the Cobden, or would be having dinner at Pharmacy restaurant in Notting Hill. Car alarms were going off along the square and down Charlotte Road, set off by people lounging on cars or pissing on them.

The Blue Note was open and people were beginning to queue up outside, waiting to be frisked for weapons and drugs. Alice and Jim had started snogging in the square at around eight-thirty, and were still at it at nine when I was convinced by the lesbian couple to join a crowd heading for the Bricklayer's Arms.

I was damned if I was going to return to the scene of my table-dancing, so I'd turned down Jon's invitation to go to dinner at Cantaloupe with the artist and the leggy blonde.

I didn't feel like going home either, so I borrowed a mobile off a pinstriped suit who asked if I was trying to chat him up. I rang Sophie but she wasn't answering. She either had her hands full dissecting her hair shafts or she was out.

At the Bricklayer's Arms the crowds were enjoying the warm evening, sprawled on the gutters and the road outside and slouching along the walls. Jake the beggar was with a crowd rolling a spliff. 'Hey, Sass babe, wait. I wanna tell you somefing,' he yelled out to me with a mouth full of food as I charged past.

In your dreams, Jake, in your dreams.

Striding past Joshua Compston's old place I was struck with a feeling of ennui. When Josh was still alive he used to hold big art events and picnics in the park. One year Damien Hirst and Angus Fairhurst had dressed up as clowns and done these splatter paintings for a pound. I still had Damien's drunken signature sprawled across our collaborative effort hanging in the loo.

I'd been offered ten thousand pounds for it by a German collector, but I'd said no. Everyone had said I was mad. It might have been a lousy scrap of paper, but it reminded me of a long hot summer when you could buy Damien Hirsts for a pound.

One year Jon, Stuart and I had run a tea shop serving Jamaican tea in tin cups, the proceeds going to the Terrence Higgins Trust. Jon and I ended up drinking far too much of the tea, a lethal mixture of pineapple juice and rum. Stuart had found us in a heap of giggles and forced us to sit under the trestle-table, where we were later joined by other inebriated reprobates.

We couldn't stop laughing and finally Stuart, exasperated beyond his usual anal behaviour, had sprayed us with rum. I couldn't get the smell out of my hair for days.

Passing Cantaloupe, I spotted Tashco at the bar, talking to someone I couldn't see because they were behind a pillar. He looked so suave sitting on the bar stool, his hair dark and slicked back behind his ears in characteristic fashion as if begging someone to come mess it up. Whoever he was with, he was making them laugh. It wasn't the leggy blonde, because I could see her at a table nearby, talking excitedly to Matt.

I knew it was a woman, though, because just as I was about to walk on, she leant in and snogged Jon something rotten. I caught sight of her long black hair as she was pulled from her chair in the embrace.

My brain contracted, expanded and wobbled, not because I had feelings other than platonic for Jon, nothing mad like that. I was just surprised. I guess the whole thing brought home to me just how far we had moved out of one another's lives. That's all.

I practically ran down to Great Eastern Street after that. I was tired from the night before, I told myself as I started shaking. Probably just feeling alone and unloved. Lunging desires, that's all it was. Hey, thirty was just around the corner – I couldn't expect to feel that brilliant.

When I got home there were two messages on my answering machine from Stuart.

'Look, I don't know where you are but I've been ringing all night. I got your note about the sale to Piers Dexter. Make sure you keep your trap shut. I don't need to tell you what confidentiality means to a man like Dexter.'

The other one just said, *'Where the fuck are you? You'd better not be at that bloody Tashco opening – if you are, you'd better start looking for another job.'*

I amended my list of things I must achieve by the time I'm thirty. I scribbled out 'Own my own gallery' and changed it to 'Be more employable'. My mother was right – I aimed too high.

My List of Favourite Pampering Methods

1 Waking up without an alarm.
2 Drinking champagne in bed with a new lover, reading art mags and watching my favourite art film ever, *How to Steal a Million* starring Audrey Hepburn.
3 Being fed peeled grapes by gorgeous men who live for me to part my lips.
4 Having my hair brushed/combed/stroked/washed by someone else.
5 Having my temperature taken.
6 Finding a vintage dress on the five-pound table at Portobello.
7 Nicking boyfriends' clothes.
8 Dreaming of lost weekends in the Prado, Guggenheim, Whitney, MOMA.
9 Getting a seat on the tube.

Sophie was stretched out in one of the chairs by the amazing Napoleon III mirror, knocking back the champagne like mad by the time I arrived at Albert's salon in St James – straight from an argument with Stuart.

Albert's salon is a v. classy affair, rococo-cum-ultra-techno. Still called Stefano's after the previous owner, it was very much the place for gorgeous young things to come to be done. Albert had added his own inimitable style to the place by offering a far more exclusive personal service – at twice the price, natch. On this occasion the salon was closed especially for Sophie's and my visit.

I was feeling frazzled and not a bit in the mood for anything other than total collapse and a pep talk *à la* Albert by the time I staggered in around four.

I had looked forward to this appointment as a chance to confront Albert about the wretched list thing, but the fight had gone out of me now. Somehow the loss of Emmanuel from my life didn't seem to matter any more – except in a pure ego sense.

Sophie was already looking a bit glassy-eyed. I noticed that the bottle of Moët looked all but empty, which made me feel slightly deflated. There is nothing worse than arriving at a venue in need of nurturing to find everyone already sloshed.

Albert's latest junior, Sal, was giving Sophie a hand

massage, wrapping her hand in a paraffin wax cast as if it was the face of Nefertiti. I was surprised he wasn't down on his knees for the act. Mind you, Sophie's hands were pretty divine. For starters, she wasn't the type of girl to gnaw her nails, unlike me.

Sal was a big black boy of about eighteen, although he looked more like twenty-five. At six feet five he had gorgeous arm muscles and the most lascivious smile I've ever seen on a fully-clothed human being. Sophie had vowed to sleep with him, even though Albert had declared him a no-fuck zone. Translate, he's mine, hands off or I'll kill you. But we weren't convinced – Sal just didn't look gay to us.

He winked at me as I dropped my old Prada bag on the trolley.

I'd finally had the big showdown thing with Stuart over curating shows of my own. Well, about everything, really. Only nothing had been achieved, natch. I would much rather have been here being wrapped in a paraffin cast by Sal.

'Well, if it isn't my favourite client!' Albert shrieked, swinging around in the chair beside Sophie to face me. Glass in one hand, fag in the other, he was the embodiment of louche but sexy with it. Albert was gangly – everything about him was long and thin, from his legs to his nose. He reminded me of a Beardsley drawing.

'With you here, Saskia, at last I feel complete.'

He says stuff like that to all his clients. I know because I've heard him, but it still had the desired effect. I felt my mood lighten.

We air-kissed, watched over by Sal, who grinned saucily at my reflection in the mirror.

I grinned inanely back.

He was rather nice, but I'd had the sauce squeezed out of me by Stuart, who had said that while he welcomed the idea of my input, the time was not right. When I asked him when it would be right, he'd muttered something under his breath that I didn't hear. I felt like saying that it was rude to mutter when you were having an important discussion with an employee, but it wouldn't have been appropriate. Besides, despite his narky phone call about going to the opening at Tashco, Stuart had been v. subdued all day. In fact, it was me on the attack for a change.

I've never really gone for confrontation, but the disquieting image of Jon snogging the unknown brunette the night before had got me worked up. Not that I was jealous or anything. It had probably just pissed me off to see another person with something happening in their life. Made me realise how blank my own future looked.

Basically I got all the stuff off my chest about wanting to curate shows. I'd even mentioned wanting a holiday in New York. Somehow, though, I felt worse than ever once I'd got it all off my chest. Stuart had looked so worn out and deflated, he hadn't even put up a fight, but pleaded with me to allow him some time to sort a few things out. Like the sucker I was, I'd nodded agreeably, but I was seething like mad inside. Time was of the essence.

'Darling,' Sophie purred at my reflection. 'You have missed the most nutritious bottle of Moet ever.' She emptied the dregs of her glass on the granite counter. She was looking at Sal as she put the glass down, and licked her lips, making the act look like an open invitation to tear off her fashion ninja outfit and screw her senseless.

Sal didn't take her up, however; he wiped his hands on his jeans and came over to me.

'I thought we agreed four o'clock,' I said, trying not to sound too petulant. Sal was air-kissing me now. He smelt like champagne and paraffin.

'Sit down, sweetie darling, and let Sal wrap your worn-out hands in one of his big pampering paraffin casts,' Albert trilled, pushing me into the seat where he had been sitting.

'I'll open another bottle, a special one I saved just for you at the back of the fridge.'

'I thought the one you opened for me was special, darling,' Sophie pouted at her reflection. Albert pinched her cheek affectionately.

'Now, now, girls, don't let those bitch hormones loose in my salon,' he soothed. 'Sal's very sensitive, aren't you, Sal?'

Sal looked lasciviously at our reflections and blew us both a kiss. We blew kisses back.

'That's better,' Albert goo-gooed. 'Sal likes it when you make nice to him, see.'

Sophie and I grinned sweetly like a couple of convent-school girls while Albert went over to the fridge and retrieved the champagne. We watched him as he made the Moët cork sigh like a virgin and giggled as he groaned suggestively. The whole performance was choreographed as carefully as a cabaret. I began to relax.

Albert always managed to make me feel like life was a glass of bubbles, and that the worst thing that could happen to me was a fit of giggles.

'If you're very good, Sassy,' he said as he poured four glasses, 'I'll let you in on some cruel gossip which I promise you will put a spring back into those fabulous legs of yours.'

'My legs aren't feeling terribly fabulous lately,' I told him, looking down at their mottled complexion.

He rolled his eyes. 'Oh, dear, are we having an attack of the cellulite blues again? If I could have ten quid for every time your legs have made me want to change camps, I'd be the richest queen in St James.'

'How cruel is the gossip, then?' I asked as he passed me a glass.

'Brutal. Torturously, toe-curlingly cruel. Now drink up while I get in character.'

'How brutal, precisely? How many reputations will be ruined?' I begged, taking a deep sip of my Moët.

'V. savage,' Sal added in his baritone, toasting me with his glass.

'And it's all about your boss, sweetie-pie,' Albert revealed, giving me a wink. 'See, Albert always knows how to please his favourite client, doesn't he?'

'Such a horrid man,' Sophie said, laying her paraffin wax cast on my hand. 'Poor Saskia.'

I nodded forlornly and took a v. deep draft of bubbles, and felt the stresses of the day drift from my body like vapour. It was gorgeous. Sal began to knead my shoulders. This was exactly the kind of treatment I needed: sympathy, champagne and massage. I purred.

Albert sat down in the seat beside me, sticking his trade-mark shiny pointed shoes on the counter. Smiling at me with one of his wicked, glinting looks that held the promise of delicious pleasure, mixed with the sweet immorality of possessing a nasty secret about someone, I began to feel v. curious. Oh, to be privy to someone else's indiscretion – these are the riches of the poor.

What could it be that Albert had on Stuart, though? I wondered as the champagne started to kick in. Boring, anal, solid as a rock Stuart – surely there were no hidden depths to discover *there*?

'Well then, are you going to dish?' I prompted him.

But Albert just went on smiling at me, his eyelashes fluttering. He was giving me a hooded look that said, 'Yes, I will give you the treasure you desire, but you're going to have to wait, my dear.'

'Oh, this is cruel,' Sophie squealed after a few minutes. She threw her head back and laughed. I noticed Sal was transfixed by her long white neck and the mane of dark hair that fell almost to the floor.

'The tension is killing us, Albert,' she moaned. 'Give it up now or I'll take to you with a pair of your own scissors.'

Sal nodded knowingly.

'I can't believe there is anything about Stuart that could possibly be that interesting,' I said. 'I mean, the man is so deeply uptight, he can't buy a loo roll without ringing up his accountant.'

'Maybe you don't know dear little Stu boy as well as you think you do,' Albert admonished.

'I've known him for six long, tedious years. I've seen him in good times and bad,' I blustered, like a vicar talking about the history of his parish.

'A *lot* of bad,' Sophie added, wrinkling her nose prettily.

Sal stopped kneading my shoulders and went back to Sophie, where he set about removing her paraffin casts. The way he gently peeled off the wax was so deeply seductive, I was sure Sophie was going to pounce on him. I couldn't believe Albert didn't comment.

'I can't believe you stayed with that bastard after how he's treated you,' Sophie remarked.

'No, darling, your masochism is too bad for words,' Albert agreed. 'You'll bring the Marquis de Sade back from the grave if you don't find your backbone soon.'

'He's not *that* bad. He's just had a rough time with Jon,' I heard myself saying.

'Oohhh, they're so *soft*,' Sophie squealed, stroking her unwrapped hands. Sal rubbed them lovingly from fingertip to armpit, even though only her hands had been softened by the wax wrap. He was definitely flirting, no doubt about it, and Sophie gave me a raised-eyebrow look to say as much, but for some reason I was feeling a bit cross now, and pretended not to have noticed her conspiratorial glance.

I refused a second glass of champagne when it was offered. 'I mean, I know he's been a bit of a pain recently, but bloody hell, his whole gallery was stripped by Jon when he left to set up Tashco,' I reminded them indignantly.

Albert refilled my glass despite my protestations and clicked his tongue in disapproval. 'OK, enough of the Poor

Stuarts or I'll put you back in therapy and start charging. We are here for pampering, goodwill and friendship this afternoon – now drink up, dear heart. I've heard nothing from you about Stuart but complaints all year. I've never met the man, but you tell me he's the biggest bastard this side of the slimeball who killed Versace, and I take your word on these things. You can't go confusing me now with poems about his virtues, girl.'

'It wasn't a poem,' I snapped.

'More of an ode, wasn't it?' Sophie teased. She was practically making love with Sal in the mirror now.

'It wasn't an ode or a poem,' I said primly, not a trace of new immorality in my voice. 'I was just saying—' but Albert didn't look like he wanted to know, and Sal and Sophie were beyond hearing. I acquiesced. 'I'm sorry,' I sighed, slumping into my chair. 'I've just had an argument with him. I don't know why I'm even defending him, you're right; he's a total arsehole,' I relented. 'So what have you got for me, Albert?'

'Dish, dish, dish,' chanted Sophie.

'Yes *dish*,' Sal ordered, 'because you've got our other piece of news to tell them as well.' He then extricated himself from Sophie and came back around to me and started back on my pampering. He squeezed a dollop of moisturiser into his palms and got to work. 'Put the dear girl out of her misery. Let's see the goods.'

'Ooohh, don't you love it when he gets all menacing and manly?' Albert asked, tickling the rippling muscles of Sal's bare tummy.

Sophie and I agreed that we did.

'Right, down to the filth. Well, a certain little shoulder-length blonde madam whose name I shan't disclose because I am the embodiment of discretion, but anyway, she's married to the owner of Wallinger's on Cork Street . . .'

'Go on, forget the tedious details, all we want is the dirt,'

Sophie demanded. I could she that she was a bit peeved over losing Sal's attention to my hands, which were now benefiting from his masterful massage techniques.

'OK, so, in the eighties when Jon Tashco and Stuart ran Bonny's on Cork Street, apparently their backer, then a certain rich banker from Switzerland whose name I will take with me to the grave, was a scammer.'

Sal rolled his eyes at me in the mirror. Now he appeared to be flirting with *me*, not that I wanted to flirt with him, but it was just his way. His whole demeanour demanded a degree of sexual play. It was just a quality he had. Still, it was pleasing to know that there were still men out there who wanted to flirt with women pushing thirty. I closed my eyes and let Albert's dirt and Sal's hands rub my tensions away.

'Anyway, apparently Stuart and Jon were using art dealing as a screen to do a spot of money-laundering.'

Sal finished massaging one hand and crossed over to start on the other. Albert poured more champagne into all of our glasses and I gulped mine down greedily. Some of the bubbles went up my nose and made me choke.

'Who's a greedy little piggy?' said Sal, winking at my reflection. I gave him an embarrassed smile.

'Apparently they were involved in a cash-for-questions wheeze, among other things.'

'That's absurd,' I snapped, jumping up hotly. Sal pushed me down.

'Go on,' Sophie demanded.

'Apparently, dirty money can be made clean by washing it in the cool waters of art. Crooks would buy a painting from Stu and Jon and then put it up for auction. Stu and Jon – for a fee, of course – would then bid the painting up sky-high on behalf of the dodgy businessman. The dirty money would be cleansed.'

'That's shit,' I said.

Sal tutted and patted my hand.

Sophie looked at me as if to say, 'What's your problem?'

Albert gave me one of his reproachful glares. 'Malicious lies maybe, but I do not dish shit out in my salon,' he snapped. He had his hands on his hips now, and I knew that if I pushed the point any further, I might end up walking out of his salon looking like Sinead O'Connor in her early years. It is written in the rule book of the new immorality that a wise girl should never argue with the man holding the comb and scissors.

'Anyway, I haven't even got to the good stuff yet, so shut up. Apparently, the backer was investigated on fraud charges and lost interest in the art market, leaving poor Stu and Jon stranded.'

'Poor dears,' sighed Sophie, trying to make eye contact with Sal. I got the feeling she was really serious about stealing him from under Albert's watchful eye, and normally I would have enjoyed waiting for the fallout, but all this rubbish about Stuart and Jon's fraud ring had made me uneasy.

'I'm sure if any of the story is true, it was nothing to do with Stuart and Jon. Anyway, I'm sure it's not true, or I would have heard something about it. I have worked for Stuart for six years.'

'It's called blind devotion, sweetie, and it doesn't sit well with your new immorality,' Albert told me.

Sal was applying the hot paraffin at that point, or I might have been tempted to give him an immoral slap in the face. Instead, I made do with a glare.

'You must admit, you do take loyalty a bit far, Sass,' Sophie said. 'I mean, what has Stuart ever done for you? After all those years at art school, your career amounts to no more than dusting crap paintings in a has-been gallery. We've just done a big spread on Cool Britannia galleries for our next issue and A SPACE isn't mentioned. Face it, darling, he's a has been and you're allowing him to hold you back.'

'Oh, and like *Class* magazine would know! Please! Your

readers think contemporary art began and ended with Monet.'

Sophie rolled her eyes. 'Give it up, Sass. Your boss doesn't give two pins for you. Why don't you start facing reality and do something for yourself for a change? Remember, you're a devotee of the new immorality. Maybe it's time you put yourself first.'

'And you'd be the expert on that, I suppose,' I snarled under my breath.

Albert hit me with his metal comb.

'Ouch!'

'Take your spats outside, girls. Anyway, let me finish, I haven't got to the filthiest bit yet. That was just the foreplay.'

'Sometimes the foreplay is the best part,' Sophie purred at Sal, but he was too busy with my hand to notice.

'Anyway, Jon and Stuart *appeared* to leave the dodgy conspiracies of Bonny's behind when they set up A SPACE.'

'See, I told you they wouldn't have been involved,' I crowed.

'Appeared to, sweetie. Use those sweet ears of yours. They only appeared to have left it behind until Stuart, dear, desperately practical boy that he is, masterminded a way to take advantage of our parliamentarians and their cash-for-questions wheeze.'

'Huh?'

'Cash for questions, darling. You know, dodgy Ministers, as in I'll give you fifty grand, you table a question for me?'

'What?' I shrieked. 'That's libel!'

'Libel's when you write it down,' Sal corrected in his calming deep baritone. Sophie blew him an approving kiss.

'That's right, Sass, as long as you don't commit pen to paper it's only scurrilous,' she said.

'That's slander,' Sal informed us.

'My, my, aren't you the little pedant,' Sophie teased, pinching Sal's butt.

I couldn't believe she'd done that, and I looked around at Albert, but he just smiled like the patriarch that he was.

'Sal's become as thick as thieves with a drop-dead-gorgeous, legs-to-her-armpits barrister,' Albert explained. 'What's her name?'

'Evelyn Hornton,' Sal told us. 'Now this girl is a walking dream,' he explained, closing his eyes and shivering with pleasure as if conjuring her image.

'A little bit struck with the legal wigged one is our Sal,' Albert explained, flicking Sal with the water off his comb.

'What? She's a nice woman, isn't she?' Sal responded, looking like he might just be prepared to go to war for this Evelyn girl, whoever she was. Some women have all the men and some, like me, have none.

'Whatever. Can I get on with my filthy rumour now?' Albert asked, hands on hips again.

My hands were set now, and I couldn't hold my glass. Albert, being the multi-talented man that he is, lifted my glass to his lips as he went on.

'You see the thing is, these politicians aren't allowed to take money for asking questions, but nothing says they can't buy art. So what they do is, they make a shrewd investment of some ne'er-do-well nobody from a dealer like Stuart Dumass, and then three months later the piece turns up at auction and goes for ten times its worth. Stuart gets a cut, the lobbyist gets his question asked and the MP gets his baksheesh. Perfect.'

'You have no proof,' I said tersely.

'Darling, I don't need proof. This is gossip, not evidence.'

'Mind you, if Stuart is investigated he'll have some pretty serious explaining to do,' Sophie remarked.

'Just remember you heard it first here, girls,' Albert reminded us, filling up our glasses.

'Come on, cheer up, sweetie, it might not happen,' he said,

noticing my glum face. Suddenly I didn't feel like drinking or having my hands massaged or my hair cut.

I was thinking of the appointment book, of the auction Stuart had run to that hadn't been entered in the diary. I cast my mind back to the desperate messages on my answerphone last night, threatening me with the sack if I spoke to anyone about the Piers Dexter purchase. I was thinking of the way Emmanuel had warned me to be careful of Stuart, and of how Jon had given me the same warning the night before. Did everyone know something I didn't? Was it really possible that I was working for a conspirator?

'What would happen if it were true and he was found guilty?' I enquired as I ran all these scenarios through my mind.

'What?' Albert asked, looking v. confused.

'If Stuart was found guilty,' I repeated, my mouth suddenly dry. 'What would happen to me? Could I be implicated?'

All three of them looked at me as if I was mad. Then at last Albert seemed to register what it was I was talking about. 'Oh, we've moved on now, Saskia,' he informed me. 'I was just telling Sophie that Sal is moving in with me. We've decided to make a serious go of it at last. Weren't you listening?'

I looked from one to the other. Sal was taking off my hand casts. Sophie was looking seriously pissed off.

I jumped out of the chair and ran.

My List of Recurring Dreams and Nightmares

1   The dream where I am running from my sister, and just
    as I am about to escape across the border I land head
    first in the chest of her husband Jeremy.
2   Damien Hirst takes holy orders and leaves the contents
    of his studio to me.
3   I'm stuck inside my duvet, the alarm clock is ringing,
    but I can't fight my way out. I end up rolling to work
    in the duvet, only to be sold as a conceptual work of
    art by Stuart.
4   I am having sex with the most perfect man alive and
    everything is pure ecstasy, when suddenly he realises
    that I am not Rebecca but her less attractive sister and
    loses his erection.
5   I find myself on the tube, where I have become the
    romantic focus of a busker who plays old Madonna hits
    on a comb. My mother is cheering him on, telling me
    not to aim so high.
6   My boss hands me an envelope and when I open it,
    eagerly expecting a pay rise, it explodes and blows all
    my hair off.
7   A really desirable man of the Piers Dexter variety goes
    on one knee to propose to me in a crowded room in front
    of my mother and sister. I tell him that while I am flattered
    by his offer, I am already married to my career. My mother
    faints just as my father walks in demanding new socks.
8   Scientists discover a cure for cellulite – but alas, my
    doctor tells me that it has come too late for me.

I justified my sudden departure from the salon by saying I'd left my tube pass in the gallery. Albert had tried to ply me with more champagne, chasing me into the street with the bottle. Sal had offered to go back to A SPACE to collect it for me, but I backed out muttering nonsense about not wanting to trouble anyone.

'I still don't believe he's gay,' Sophie had hissed in my ear as we kissed goodbye. 'Did you see the way he was flirting with me? God, the boy was drooling.'

Unlike me, Sophie didn't believe that any man was gay. In my experience, nine out of ten men are gay. The rest are married or enduring a long prison sentence for rape/murder, etc. Sophie had a belief in her ability to seduce all men regardless of which camp they thought they were in. Her self-esteem challenged almost every late nineties book on single girls and their propensity to cellulite-gaze.

But that afternoon, as I ran through the peak hour, pedestrians erupting all over St James, I wasn't thinking of cellulite or self-esteem.

I had to find out if Albert's gossip was true. For starters, I had to know if was I going to end up in prison before my thirtieth birthday.

I could hear my mother now, making pronouncements about how I was always the plain one, and how my lack of marriageable qualities had led to my downfall. Even Martin the Buddhist would be ashamed of me. He'd no doubt regale his monkish pals with my excessive love of chocolate and my inability to steer the middle path.

As I shoved my way through the crowds leaving work for the day, I wasn't sure who could give me the answers I needed. Let's face it, I couldn't just confront Stuart. He would waffle his way out of it if it was true, or fire me if it wasn't.

That left Jon. Maybe that was why he'd left A SPACE. Maybe it was nothing to do with Petri dishes and bubonic plague, after all, and he was simply afraid of being implicated in Stuart's crime ring. And maybe the artists that went with him knew something, too. Was that what Emmanuel had warned me about? Did everyone know except me? I held my head as I ran.

My conjecture had to be cut short as, just as I was about to turn into Bond Street, I charged head first straight into the chest of Piers Dexter.

'Hello,' he laughed, picking my v. embarrassed face out of his suit. I got a heavy blast of his cologne up my nose, something I couldn't name, mingled with a sexy all-man aroma that I could. I wanted to ask him back to my flat for sex, but, as per normal, I wasn't up for rejection.

'What's the rush?' he drawled as he checked his shirt, for stains no doubt. There was a lipstick smear on his collar. Whoops.

'No rush,' I told him, panting hard and loud. 'I just realised that I left my tube pass in the gallery and I was running back to get it before Stuart left.' I looked at him innocently, deciding to stick with the lie I'd prepared earlier for Albert and Co.

'Well, I think you may be too late. I just passed by on the off chance myself. I was hoping to arrange the collection of my paintings, but it was all locked up at A SPACE. Don't they give you a key?'

'They?' I said, my mind swirling with fraud conspiracy theories. As far as I was concerned, Dexter was very much in the frame as a suspect. I mean, no one could seriously have liked 'White Mood Swing', could they? What was the bet those paintings ended up at auction sooner rather than later?

'Stuart, your boss?' he prompted. 'Doesn't he trust you with a key?'

'You said *they*,' I reminded him, feeling quite the little detective now. It's amazing how, even in the twenty-first century, conspiracy theories can really take a hold of a normally level-headed girl. OK, so maybe level-headed was pushing it a bit. But seriously, the minute something weird happens, my whole rational edifice, such as it is, falls apart.

'Did I?' he asked, a veritable picture of guilelessness. Not that I was taken in for a second, natch.

'Yes. How long have you known Stuart?' I demanded, the inspector within me taking over. I gave him a probing, all-knowing stare.

'I spoke to him on the phone the day I met you. Listen, is everything all right?' he asked, looking a bit bewildered by my intensity and shrewd questioning.

'Perfect,' I told him primly, gazing squarely into his eyes, which I now noticed were v. blue indeed. They were the colour of an Yves Klein painting, a spectacular Yves Klein blue. I began to feel quite Holly Golightlyish all of a sudden. Then I reminded myself that thirty per cent of all criminally insane people have blue eyes.

Dexter's eyes were the colour of the Red Sea, and for a minute there I almost felt like diving in for a quick snorkel. I looked away for fear of being hypnotised. They really were dreamy as far as big blue eyes with long dark lashes go – if you go for that sort of thing. I squared my shoulders to show that I wasn't the sort of girl to drown in the eyes of a conspirator like him. 'I'm so OK, I'm dangerous,' I warned him.

He laughed. 'Is that why you're wearing a plastic poncho?' he enquired, pointing at my torso.

Ouch!

I looked down at the silver wrap with white trim which Sal had attached to me moments before I'd rushed out of the salon. It had the words *I'm a Bolly Boy in a Bolly World!* embroidered on the front. One of Albert's old boyfriends had made it specially. V. embarrassing.

'Oh *this*?' I laughed, pointing to the poncho. 'Well, I, well, you see there was . . .' I stuttered, running through a few likely explanations in my head.

After a few more ums, ers and well you sees, I had to concede that there was no explanation. Then again, perhaps there was no point in explaining. Let's face it, Piers Dexter wasn't really after a plausible excuse so much as a laugh at my expense. He was falling apart at the seams at the hilarity of it all, in fact.

'I'm sorry, Saskia, I shouldn't laugh,' he howled, somewhat pointlessly.

'Be my guest,' I told him sarcastically as I folded my arms across my chest and pretended to be v. bored rather than embarrassed.

A few passers-by, hearing his guffaws, stopped to check out the joke and after a few seconds a crowd began to gather to chuckle at the little free sideshow I was offering. One smart-arse even read out the *I'm a Bolly Boy!* slogan for those with poor eyesight.

Humiliated beyond my wildest dreams, I started to make my farewells but Dexter, the bastard, pulled me back. This was worse than my nightmare of being told that the cure for cellulite has come too late for me; worse even than the nightmare where I can't find my way out of my duvet and roll into work in it.

'Look,' he said, dragging me into a Tudor doorway, away from the intensity of the crowd. Some of them were getting a bit testy, demanding more than a mere plastic poncho for their entertainment. 'At least let me get you a cab home.'

'No, really, it's fine,' I told him, smiling stiffly. 'It's quicker on the tube.'

'But you left your pass at work,' he reminded me.

'I think my budget can stretch to a tube ticket.' I pulled away.

'Forget it,' he insisted. 'I know what those ticket queues are like at this time of day.'

'Really?' I asked, before I could stop myself. 'I wouldn't have had you down as a public transport man.' I gave a little self-satisfied simper, as if public transport was somehow beyond the capabilities of Piers Dexter.

'Why? Do you think it's beyond my capabilities?' he riposted archly, making me feel like a bitch as well as a public joke.

'No, not that,' I lied, realising again how handsome he was. He had one of those ski tans that I'd always made fun of in the past. 'I just thought you could afford to avoid it, that's all,' I replied diplomatically.

'I don't always avoid things just because I can afford to, Saskia,' he replied.

I could see I'd cut him to the quick. I hung my head.

'Come on, where do you live?' he asked, lifting my chin. I don't know why, but, for a second I thought he was going to snog me.

I felt my teeth rattling around in my head with nerves as I replied, 'Notting Hill, but don't worry about it.'

'Ditto,' he said, grinning broadly. 'See, we're neighbours. We can share a cab.'

I stood by, resigned to my fate, and watched from the kerb as he hailed a cab and told the driver where to take us. He ushered me into the cab and then sat on one of the pull-down seats opposite me.

I kept blushing every time his bespoke foot touched my

Israeli army-issue boot. But he didn't seem to notice. He chatted away happily, telling me how much he missed New York and the compactness of it all. How, while he loved London, he found the constant drizzle a bit depressing.

He told me about his house on Ladbroke Square, and how his two Burmese cats had scratched their way through to the stuffing of his sofa and were now hard at work destroying his Dinos and Jake Chapman sculpture. He told me about how he hated flying Concorde, and how he loved Paris and owned a chateau just outside the city.

I listened, feeling like Little Orphan Annie as he gave his dissertation on how the other half of Notting Hill live. His cats probably enjoyed more of the high life than I did.

Not that I'm a socialist or anything – well, no more than anyone else without money is. Let's face it, the redistribution of wealth seems like a neat idea when you have nothing personally to redistribute apart from a plastic poncho and a soggy pair of vintage shoes.

Let's just say I was envious.

I don't think he was trying to impress me or anything sad like that – he knew I wasn't in the mood to offer much in the way of conversation back, so he was doing all the talking. At least he avoided all those annoying probing questions which would have seriously pissed me off, given my current circumstances. Questions about what I'm doing, who I was and where I was going in life. Questions for which I had no answers. Just lists.

As he spoke, he sort of hunched over as if we were sharing a secret, and as we crawled along Bayswater Road, I began to wish we were travelling further afield – to Heathrow even, or to his chateau in France. Only we'd have to stop somewhere along the way and buy me some clothes to replace the *Bolly Boy* poncho, natch.

I envisaged the two of us walking hand in hand along the beach at Cannes in our fabulously expensive espadrilles, not caring a bit whether the tide was destroying them because we had a hundred pairs just like them back at the villa.

I was startled back to reality by Piers, mimicking the way his cats cried. I couldn't help laughing. I realised then that he was making me like him. He was ensuring his place in my affections by his affability and endearing self-deprecation.

I was relaxing, and not remembering to be suspicious of his connection to Albert's rumours. Either the man had *the* most appalling taste this side of the river, or he had bought the Jeff Hewit show to auction it. I was in lust either with a crook or a rich bloke with no taste. Neither was that appealing.

Just the same, I was flirting outrageously by the time he asked me which street I lived on. I described which end of Pembridge Villas to go to as if I were giving directions to my bedroom. I had more or less decided that I would like to sleep with him. He had only to give the signal.

I was a bit peeved, therefore, when the cab stopped outside my flat and Piers made no move to press me to go for a drink or dinner or to bed with him.

'So, then. Maybe you'll drop around sometime tomorrow to arrange collection,' I suggested hopefully as he got back into the cab and closed the door.

'Sure,' he agreed, opening the cab driver's divide and giving him his address. I stood there lamely hoping he was going to change his mind and press his company on me for a bit longer. When the cab drove off I waited for him to turn back and wave. But he didn't, and I felt more tragic than ever. I would add, 'Never wait on the kerb for a man to wave goodbye' to my list of things I must not do again.

It wasn't until I got inside the entrance to our block of flats that I realised I was still wearing the silver poncho. I suppose I should be grateful that Piers Dexter hadn't amused himself at my expense by saying 'Bye, Bolly Boy', or something humiliating like that.

Alice wasn't back, so I played my messages. There was one from my mother, urging me to ring Rebecca.

You never ring her and she thinks it's because you're afraid of intruding. You know she doesn't want to make you feel inadequate just because you have had no luck with men. You're her flesh and blood, after all. She said if you like you can come to dinner on Saturday – she'll invite one of Jeremy's work colleagues. Wouldn't that be nice, dear?'

'Dream on, Rebecca,' I said to myself as I rewound the machine to play the messages that Stuart had left the night before, about what secrecy meant to men such as Dexter. As Stuart's irritated voice filled the flat, I started writing a list of all the things I hated about Piers Dexter, starting with his name. In reality, I was annoyed with myself for fancying a man who didn't fancy me back.

When Alice came home I went over Albert's rumour with her. She agreed with me that there was probably no foundation to his story at all and that I should forget it. But I couldn't stop torturing her with it. I went over and over it with her while she shampooed, conditioned and dried her hair. She finally got the red out after several washes.

Jim hadn't noticed the change at all as it turned out, and now Alice had decided to drop him. Why did all my friends have such strength of purpose where men were concerned, while I was such a spineless pushover? I asked Alice, but she just held the hairdryer to my face.

'I can't believe you are giving any credence to gossip you heard in Albert's salon,' she yelled over the roar of the drier. 'I mean, he's always dishing on someone, that's why he's such fun. You're not meant to take it seriously. I'm sure he'd be destroyed to think you actually believed anything he said. All his stories come from his mad clients, you know.'

'Yeah, I guess,' I agreed.

'If you like, I can ask Jon about it,' she suggested. 'I'm sure he would have a perfectly logical explanation.'

'No, don't do that!' I yelped, a little more urgently than I meant to.

List of Things that Prove a Girl's Growing Purpose and Maturity

1   Asking a guy in for coffee, drinking coffee and then sending him home.
2   Starting a pension plan.
3   Owning up to a guy that you fancy him.
4   Waking up without an alarm clock.
5   Investing a month's salary on an original artwork
6   Acting, not reacting to pressures.
7   Not faking orgasms or at least owning up afterwards when you do.
8   Giving regularly to a favourite charity. (This does not mean having sex with destitute artists.)
9   Not entering people's names on my hit list just because they annoy me.
10   Buying clothes that fit.

The next day at work was hideous beyond belief. Stuart was testy all morning and gave me dire chores to do, such as dusting, sweeping and filing. V. demeaning.

I toyed very seriously with the idea of handing in my notice – only not seriously enough to actually do it, natch. Instead I vented my frustrations by updating my hit list, re-entering the name Stuart Dumass several more times.

Far from sending me off for another lunch break as I'd been hoping (I still had to find the outfit that was going to make Emmanuel eat his intestines with regret about dumping me), Stuart had disappeared at around two in the afternoon, leaving me in charge of the gallery.

He had been wearing that I-might-run-off-and-join-the-Moonies look when he announced that he had another auction to go to. I had to bite my tongue to stop myself from exposing my suspicions.

As soon as he walked out of the door I was leafing through that diary like a wife going through her husband's pockets. Sure enough, right after an early entry about the purchase of a bottle of disinfectant for cleaning the sinks, and a note about a phone call to a dealer in New York, there was a conspicuous blank. Basically the word *auction* was significant only in its absence.

The realisation that Albert's insinuations might be true hit me hard. More so because I'd basically allowed myself to be convinced by Alice that there was no substance to them. Something inside me broke. It was as if the constant trickle of disillusionment dripping into my life had become a deluge.

I simply couldn't take it any more, and to make my fate aware of this fact I let out a long, loud wail of emotional despair, sort of like women do on television serials when told that their husband has been murdered, or rebirthing people do when they realise that they were a forceps delivery.

The noise that came out of me was truly terrible but v. satisfying. I'd never really realised how deep I was before, and refreshed, I tried it again. It was the sort of gut-wrenching howl that girls who have been unlucky in love, looks, thighs, career and, well, most things really, tend to make when they find that they are on the brink of the ageing process. Soon I was going to be all those things listed above *and* wrinkly. It was too much to bear in silence.

I was just rounding off the last wail when I realised that Piers Dexter had managed to sneak in and was now standing in front of me, white as the proverbial 'White Mood Swing'.

'Are you all right?' he asked as his shadow fell across the diary.

'All right?' I repeated, slowly lifting my eyes to face him.

Funnily enough my outburst had left me a bit stuck for words. But poor Piers looked v. concerned and I felt it necessary to reassure him that what he'd just witnessed wasn't anything to trouble himself about.

I swallowed hard. This was going to be harder to explain than the plastic poncho.

At first, drawing a blank in the plausible explanation department, I did one of my fish impersonations for a bit – which didn't seem to settle his concerns much at all. If anything, he looked even more worried.

He reached out and touched me gently on the shoulder. It felt v. soothing, and I closed my eyes dreamily. I didn't want him to stop. 'Yes, are you all right? That wailing just then. It sounded like a cry of pain. Hell of a noise. I thought you were being murdered – so did most of Bond Street, by the way. What happened?'

I grasped my throat.

'Murdered?' I said.

His brow was furrowed with concern. He really did look worried, poor thing, and my state of acute embarrassment was finally superseded by a need to put his mind at rest. Years of being let down by my horoscope had made me great at mood changes.

'No, no, no,' I chuckled, rolling my eyes at his misapprehension. 'That noise you just heard me make then? Is that what you mean? You thought I was in pain?'

He nodded.

'No, no, no. That? It was just a life-affirming howl of delight. I took a course on Life Affirming Cries of Delight at Glastonbury last year, see. V. therapeutic, actually, if you have the time and the lung capacity. I can highly recommend them.' Oh, God, what was I blabbering about?

'What?' he asked, as if he didn't believe a word of it.

'A Life Affirming Howl of Delight course,' I repeated, digging myself in further.

He didn't look convinced.

'Well, a spontaneous yelp of happiness if you like. A bit like Chelsea fans do when one of their own scores a goal. You should see them in the stands, screaming their heads off. A mass wail of oneness with all things Chelsea. A cry of the inner self as it embraces existence. You know the thing, letting it all hang out and connection with the divine.'

Piers Dexter shook his head and said that he wasn't familiar with any of those concepts at all.

'You've heard guys yelling their heads off at baseball matches?' I asked, hoping to break the concept down for him.

He nodded that he did know those guys, but said he couldn't see how that related to the noise he'd just heard me making.

Work with me, Piers, I wanted to say. 'You must have yelled your head off once in a while?' I prompted.

'Not like that, no.'

'You should. It's marvellous. Better than E. And afterwards you feel all at peace with your chi.'

He shook his head. 'Chi?'

'Life force?'

He kept up the head-shaking, mystified. He was really going to make me work for this explanation. In the end I decided there was nothing for it, I was going to have to give a repeat performance. I put my head back and let out another incredible yell, although without quite the same degree of pathos this time.

I followed the yell with a series of loud whooping sounds and punched the air with my fist. My throat was getting a bit scratched and raw by the end of it.

'See, nothing but sheer exuberance,' I assured him, bouncing up and down to show him the sort of feisty feelings a life-affirming noise like that could evoke in a girl.

'Seriously?' he asked.

'Seriously,' I promised, repeating the noise once more, only without quite so much of the fist-thrusting this time. God, I was a mess. All this stuff was definitely going on the list of Behaviour to be Avoided after Thirty.

'So, everything's OK? He was still looking pretty dubious about it all, although at least he was smiling agreeably now – even if he did suspect I had blown a chip.

'You've got it,' I assured him. 'I can hardly believe how all right things are. And you,' I asked. 'Are you all right?' I followed up my enquiry with a hearty punch on his arm.

He looked at his arm as if I might have left a sticky mark, but then he breathed out a bit and seemed to relax. Maybe the memory of yesterday and the poncho was coming back to him, because a big smile spread across his face and next second he was laughing. 'I'm fine,' he chuckled. 'God, Saskia, you're mad. So what was it that led to all this?'

'What?'

'Your spontaneous life-affirming howl? What evoked the need for hooting and wailing? It must have been something pretty amazing.'

'Um . . .' Now he had me. I felt my brain squirm up with the stress of it all. 'Yes, you're right, it was,' I agreed, casting around my mental tool kit for an excuse. 'My, er, sister has invited me to dinner on Saturday night. That's what it was,' I told him. Had I actually said that? Bloody hell, I *was* desperate.

He looked bewildered. 'Are you very close, then?' he enquired as if he thought it v. unlikely.

'Terribly,' I lied. I held crossed fingers up to demonstrate the strength of our closeness. 'We are practically soulmates,' I assured him. 'A girl couldn't hope for a better sister.'

'Well that's fantastic,' he remarked, still looking troubled.

'It is,' I agreed, warming to my lie, but then I went and spoilt the effect by blabbering on about how she had invited a friend of her husband's for me to meet.

He looked v. horrified now. 'A blind date?' he spluttered, as if I'd just owned up to being an avid thimble collector. 'An actual blind date? Do people still put themselves through those?'

'Um, well, I suppose it is. Not that I care about that aspect of it, obviously. Blind date? Give me a break, definitely not,' I scoffed. 'I just like seeing her, really, and her husband needs a friend to talk to while I'm there, so that he doesn't feel too left out. My sister and I tend to exclude others when we're together because of our closeness, you see. She had to get Jeremy to bring a friend so it wouldn't be too dull for him.'

He raised one eyebrow. 'That's very touching,' he said. 'I try to avoid my sister when I can. She lives in Indiana. She's married to a rich grain farmer who drives a tractor all day. He's the size of a house and she's getting that way,' he added, puffing his cheeks up to put me in the picture.

'My sister is very attractive,' I gabbled, trying to dig myself out of this absurd conversation. How was I ever going to make him want to have sex with me now? This was dreadful. 'She's married to a merchant banker, actually,' I told him, thinking that my mother couldn't have marketed Rebecca better herself.

'Well, that's a pity because I was going to ask you if you'd join me for dinner on Saturday night.'

'Dinner? Me? Oh,' I sighed, as if someone had just stuck a pin in me.

'I should have asked earlier, I guess. Maybe some other time, then?'

'What about tonight?' I suggested before I realised what I'd done. I mean, no self-respecting girl under thirty accepts a date at such short notice, let alone proposes one herself. This was tragic.

No matter how sad and desperate her love life, a girl must never appear so available as to suggest that she has nothing better to do on a Friday night. It goes hand in hand with being friendless and unlovable – a thimble collector. Now he would think that my life was empty and uneventful. He was probably considering what a good chum I'd make for his sister in Indiana.

'You mean you don't have something else on?'

At least he seemed surprised. Either that, or he was mortified that he had invited someone so sad out on a date. 'Well, I do have other plans, you know. It's not that I have nothing else on – heavens no. That couldn't be further from the truth. I've got engagements coming out of my ears. Openings, parties, clubs. My friends have been on the phone begging me to go out with them all day.'

Piers Dexter looked at me oddly. I sensed that the plastic poncho and the smudged lipstick memories were vying for his attention again. His eyes were heralding an impending fit of laughter. Or maybe those were tears about to spring forth? Maybe he was about to weep with sympathy at how pathetic I was.

Just as I was about to climb into the bottom drawer of the filing cabinet, he spoke. 'Seven OK?' he asked.

'Seven?'

'I'll pick you up at your place, shall I?'

I closed the filing cabinet drawer and smiled up at him sexily. 'Oh right, yes, definitely. Flat six, it's up five flights of stairs and don't mind the smell, it's just that the people downstairs have a baby,' I ranted. 'And watch your suit or whatever on the pushchair device in the lobby, it's a bit of a squeeze. And if the Polish woman in the red scarf comes out, just push past her without speaking or she'll have you in for a tarot reading.'

'Sounds colourful at your place,' he said. I suppose that was his polite way of saying it sounded like a tenement.

'It is. I mean, it is interesting. It's not social housing or anything, no one there is on benefit,' I prattled on. 'The couple with the baby run a PR company and the Polish woman, well, she might be on benefit but anyway she's lived there for ever and the gay guys below us are writers. One of them's sort of famous in a local sense.'

Piers was laughing again and I felt my cheeks go bright red.

'It's only you I'll be picking up,' he explained.

I went into crisp, professional mode as if the last ten minutes hadn't happened. 'Right. See you at seven, then. I'll let my friends know I won't be able to make it. They'll be disappointed obviously.'

The phone rang as he left the gallery and I lunged on it, hoping it was Stuart telling me that he was out at Safeway, buying loo roll, and would I mind noting it in his diary. But it wasn't.

'Stuart Dumass, please.' The caller had a hard, gravelly voice with a strong accent, maybe cockney, or foreign even – it was difficult to tell. I told him that Stuart was out and asked if he'd like me to take a message.

'Tell him the job's done and that I'll meet him tonight.'

'I'll just write that down,' I told him. 'Who should I say called?'

'No need for a name, he'll know what it's about. You be a good girl and tell him to be there. Usual place. Tell him I've got what he wants. He should find it very interesting.'

After I put the phone down I realised that I had to get out of there. This whole scenario was getting a tad out of hand. Without even bothering to grab my bag, I ran out of the gallery to the station in a complete state. I even bought a piece of heather from an Irish woman who told me it could remove curses. That's what I was, cursed; but looking at the dead purple flowers I doubted even a whole caravan of gypsies could help.

As the train rattled along and I hung from my strap watching subterranean London, I tried to remember if I had put the latch on and set the burglar alarm. I told myself that one did things like that automatically and pushed it from my mind. I was always worrying about stuff like that. I ran home from work once a month certain that I'd left the gas on, only to get there and discover we had no gas appliances. Without my lists I'd forget everything.

A busker who'd come to sing an old Oasis song got spooked by the way I was staring at my heather sprig and muttering to myself about conspiracy theories. Eventually he lost his bottle, fudged his lines and went off to another carriage without even bothering to pass the hat around.

When I got out at Old Street, I charged across the heavy traffic on Great Eastern Street and down Charlotte Road. Someone I knew called out to me but I didn't stop. I just kept going until I pushed through the glass doors of Tashco. Jon was standing near the door and I fell into his arms.

'It's Stuart,' I cried, gasping for breath. 'It's Stuart, he, he, he, he's in some kind of trouble. Albert says it's a conspiracy. Oh, what am I going to do Jon, what am I going to do?'

He wrapped me up in his arms and kissed me on the head. I heard him ask Alice to go to Cantaloupe and get me a whisky.

'Is it true?' I asked, pulling myself out of his warm, now slightly damp chest and looking up into his eyes. 'Jon, tell me it's not true. Is it?'

He pressed my head back into his chest and started to kiss my hair again. He was murmuring things like, 'There, there' and 'Don't cry' and 'I'm here', and I didn't want him to stop – not ever. Even though I was bereft and practically hysterical, being kissed by Jon like that was making me feel nicer than I'd ever felt in all my life.

'I didn't want you of all people to find out, Saskia. Oh God, you've got to believe me, I didn't want you to find out,' he said, and then he said it again. It was v. soothing.

I snuggled closer into his shirt until I could feel his nipples. Suddenly Stuart was the furthest thing from my mind. I looked up and said something soap-opera-ish like 'Oh, Jon!' and that was when he started snogging me.

Essential Night-time Rituals

1 Read *The Shock of the New!* By Robert Hughes – my art bible.
2 Listen to my body clock – I figure I won't feel like a whole woman until I hear it.
3 Follow a useless beauty tip from a magazine that promises an end to split ends/cellulite/spots.
4 Brush my hair a hundred times and try not to notice how much comes out in the brush.
5 Insert ear plugs (so I don't have to hear Alice's love life).
6 Put on eye mask (don't want to see that I don't have a love life of my own).
7 Take sleeping pills – for when I can't get thoughts of why no one wants to sleep with me out of my head.
8 Resist temptation to eat toast in bed.
9 Distract myself by re-evaluating my list of dreams.
10 Eat toast in bed.

Alice came back with the whisky just as we'd pulled apart for fear of ending up like those dogs you see mating on the street. Stuck together, waiting for a Good Samaritan to throw a bucket of water over them.

She wasn't a fool, though. I think she knew that more than a few supportive pats on the back had passed between us in her absence.

She gave me my whisky and I drank it down eagerly.

'She's upset about some stupid rumour that her hairdresser Albert told her,' she explained to Jon.

'There's more to it now,' I added, keen to avoid being labelled neurotic. I didn't want Jon to think of me as one of those old women who gets easily rattled. There was a woman who lived in Horsham who used to ring the emergency services every time the gas man called to read the meter. 'I took a phone call for Stuart from some guy who wouldn't give his name.'

'It was probably an insurance salesman,' she said. 'They go through the phone book.'

'No, it wasn't!'

'What do you think, Jon?' Alice asked.

Jon wasn't commenting.

'You don't understand,' I insisted. 'He was very shifty. I can't explain it but it was the way he spoke. It was v.

menacing, actually. He said that he had something for Stuart that would interest him.'

Alice threw her hands in the air in a what-did-I-say gesture. 'See! Definitely an insurance salesperson – I bet he has an endowment policy he wants Stuart to buy,' she suggested knowledgeably.

Thankfully Jon put the brakes on her theory. He looked about as taken with it as I was. 'Alice, do you think you can look after things here? I think I'll take Saskia out for a bit. Whatever's going on, she's shaken up about it.'

He was rubbing my back as he said this, and I was practically swooning with his touch. How could I have ignored these feelings for Jon for so long, I wondered, as Alice agreed and gave me a big hug.

'Honestly, Sass, I'm sure it's nothing. Albert's just winding you up. Don't read too much into it, OK?'

'Sure,' I nodded, no longer considering Stuart or Albert or anyone other than Jon as he led me out to his car – a smart white BMW. I didn't stop to consider that last time I'd been for a drive with Jon it had been in an old Citroën with a hole in the floor you could see the road through.

We drove down to St John Street in Clerkenwell to one of those trendy offal-type restaurants that guarantees the quality of their meat, and if you mention BSE they look at you as if you're too uncool to go on living.

Jon ordered a huge plate of bone marrow, but I didn't feel like eating. I was a bit confused after the kiss, and my stomach felt as full as my head felt empty. It was a bit of a shock having something that had once been on my wish list, more or less, actually come true. Then the image of Jon kissing the girl in Cantaloupe the other night started zigzagging through my brain.

I had to pull myself together and not read too much into it. I went down into my deeper self and restrained my desires. The sceptic in me told me that kissing Jon was merely an aberration, a freak accident that meant nothing. As if Jon and I could ever have a future together. As if.

I tried to settle my libido with logical arguments about how Jon was probably just being friendly and got carried away in the moment. After all, I was practically slobbering over his nipples while I was sobbing all over his chest. Nipples are meant to be the third most potent erogenous zone on a man's body. Why, I'd practically seduced him when you thought about it.

Jon probably saw that snogging me senseless was the best way to calm me down. Much better than a pat on the back, and not nearly as distressing for the customers as slapping me across the face.

Jon and I were friends – how could I think otherwise? It must be turning thirty that was doing this to me. Sometimes friends got carried away, that was natural, especially in the age of the new immorality. Didn't mean anything. Jon was a gorgeous man, and all that. A girl would have to be seriously dense not to find him sexy, but we'd been down the romantic involvement path before and decided that it wasn't for us.

A snog was a snog was a snog, I told myself poetically. I had to steel myself for the inevitability that it meant nothing more.

Jon had squeezed my hand at one point on the journey to the restaurant, but that was more in a brotherly/friend kind of way. There was nothing in his demeanour now to suggest that he was planning another assault on my lips.

Even as I thought this, though, my heart was pounding. Just grow up and act your age, Saskia Williams, I scolded myself as I watched him shovelling the bone marrow onto his fork with his knife. 'Don't let him slip through your fingers now,' my mother's voice riposted.

'Are you all right, Saskia? You seem to be muttering.'

I was startled into consciousness. 'What?'

'You were muttering something about your fingers.'

'Oh. I was visiting my deeper self. I do that sometimes.'

Jon nodded doubtfully. 'So tell me: what was it that Albert said?' he asked casually, just as the waiter came to take his plate. He hadn't mentioned the cause of my distress before that; we'd more or less limited ourselves to general topics. Jon had asked me if I was still making my lists, and I had told him that actually I'd just been updating my hit list before the weird guy rang up.

Jon laughed and shook his head. 'I remember that hit list. I used to take a peek at it whenever I thought you might be cross with me,' he confided.

'God! I'd never put *you* on it!' I shrieked.

We laughed and Jon squeezed my hand in such a warm, affectionate kind of way that I knew everything was going to be OK. Maybe he'd even ask me to come and work with him again, I hoped at one point, before my loyalty to Alice forced me to chase the rogue idea from my mind.

He reached out and touched my ear and I blushed crimson.

'I'm sure Alice is right,' I told him, trying to sound composed. 'I've probably got the wrong end of the stick. It wouldn't be the first time. Albert is always getting me in a mess. Only last week he orchestrated the utter ruination of my relationship with Emmanuel.'

Jon laughed so hard that the ash from his cigarette fell onto the table. 'Well that was no great loss; Emmanuel was the biggest jerk in the long list of jerks you've dated. I applaud this Albert guy if that's the effect he has on your life.'

I blushed some more, quite pleased that Jon held an opinion about the guys I dated. Naturally it was just a brotherly opinion, and I wasn't going to read too much into it.

'Emmanuel *was* an aberration,' I agreed. 'But I'm almost thirty, Jon. In less than three weeks' time, in fact. Now is not the time to be losing boyfriends,' I explained. 'Ask my mother. They get harder and harder to find after the big Three-0.'

He laughed. The cigarette was still in his mouth, and I thought it wasn't possible that there could be a sexier man. Everything he did was so cool. It seemed extraordinary to me now that I hadn't done something about ravishing Jon sooner. All those wasted years when I hadn't acknowledged my feelings for him seemed like a black hole of wasted time. But just as I was about to fall blissfully in love, the image of him kissing the girl in Cantaloupe ran like a streaker across the pitch of my brain again.

'I really don't think you need worry about the availability of boyfriends, Saskia. Believe me, as a man about to hit the big Four-0, you have nothing to worry about.' Then he took my hand, turned it over and ran his finger meaningfully over my palm as he gazed into my eyes.

It was the most erotic experience I've ever had at a restaurant table, even counting the time I had full sex under a table at Pharmacy twelve months ago.

'What was it Albert said, exactly?' he insisted, still gazing into my eyes.

'Who?' I said, mesmerised by the fine laugh lines that fanned out from the corners of his eyes. I was wondering if I should take the initiative and pull him under the table now, but there was a waiter watching us who I suspected was harbouring similar fantasies about Jon.

'Albert,' he repeated. 'What did he actually tell you about Stuart? You never told me the details.'

'Oh,' I said, rather disappointed that we were back onto Stuart. I mean, I know I had been absolutely manic about it earlier, but here among the offal and the wine, feeling all sexy and desirous of Jon, Stuart and his dodgy dealings were the last things I wanted to focus on. I was feeling much more in the mood for passionate kisses.

Still, Jon was just trying to help, I told myself. Just trying to be caring and sharing and wonderfully sensitive. So I gave him the story from the beginning, including all the details about the auctions Stuart kept popping out to. Jon nodded sagely when I mentioned the significance of these outings not being recorded in the diary. He was so gorgeous and wonderful, it was all I could do not to snog him.

Jon nodded the whole way through my story, asking for the odd detail here and there but for the most part letting me get on with it. I couldn't remember anyone ever being so interested in what I had to say. Apart from Piers, although that was because he found me such an oddball.

Towards the end, I thought he looked a bit annoyed when I brought up my idea about going to the police. But that was only natural. I mean, Jon probably felt a sense of loyalty to Stuart after all their years together. It just showed what a sweet man he was, and anyway he cheered up considerably when I explained that I didn't imagine for a minute that anyone would think *he* was involved.

'Don't forget that Albert heard all this from the wife of some gallery owner. Probably just a bitch causing trouble. And even if the Swiss guy who backed you all those years was involved, I'm sure you knew nothing about it and if you did, you had nothing to do with it. That's why you left Cork Street in the first place and set up A SPACE, isn't it?'

Jon nodded.

'I see now that you had to leave A SPACE. Although at the time, I have to say, I thought you were a bastard.'

He leant across the table then and kissed me on the nose. As he pulled away the waiter arrived with the dessert menu, but feeling all strengthened by Jon's kiss, I turned up my freshly adored nose at offers of bread-and-butter pudding and the like and opted for a double espresso.

'Was there anything else?' Jon asked when the waiter had taken our order. 'I mean, there was no mention at all of my being involved?' He was squeezing my hand so tightly that

I began to worry that my nails – such as they were – might drop off.

The poor love must have been furious at having such absurd accusations hurled around when he'd done everything he could to distance himself from Stuart's scam. Just the same, my hand really was hurting.

I reassured him that there was nothing to worry about. 'Clearly the rumour was more to do with Stuart. Albert didn't mention you directly at all. It was all about Stuart running some sort of cash-for-questions racket, which sounds highly unlikely given Stuart's hatred of politics, don't you think? He didn't even vote for New Labour when Blair was talking about all those lovely things they were going to do for the arts.'

'So he didn't mention my name in connection with the scam at all?' Jon probed as if he hadn't been listening to a word I said.

'Only in the sense that you were running the Cork Street gallery with him, but I'm sure you weren't actually involved in anything underhand.' I gave a little chuckle to show him how utterly unbelievable I thought the idea was. 'How ludicrous.'

He didn't seem to find it so funny. He pulled away from my hand and began running his fingers through his hair. He had those long, tapered fingers that make everything they do look like the stylised gestures of a Thai dancer. 'You have to understand that I can't have any of this shit landing on Tashco. Not now. You have to promise me that you won't bring this up with Stuart,' he said.

I laughed. 'Are you kidding? I can't even bring up my lunch break with Stuart. Since you left, I hardly dare speak to him at all. This is definitely not something I want to discuss with him. I can just see his face, were I to ask him was he involved in a money-laundering ring. Yeah, right.' I rolled my eyes.

'Promise me,' he insisted, using his fingers to squeeze my hand again until it hurt.

'Of course not,' I agreed, pulling my hand away a bit. 'Only, please tell me what's going on.'

'I don't want you in on this, Saskia,' he said quite firmly. 'That was why I wanted you to come to work at Tashco with me. Oh shit, I wish you'd never stayed at A SPACE and got mixed up in all this.'

I dropped my head and inhaled the steam from the espresso which had just been put down in front of me. My Regrets list was seriously mounting up now. Why did I have such a knack for doing the wrong thing? Of course I should have gone to work for Jon, instead of staying with the sergeant major of London art.

If I had gone to Tashco, I would be the girl dyeing my hair red on a whim and chucking men at the drop of a hat. Instead I was roaming St James in plastic ponchos making tragic, old-maid-type suggestions to Piers Dexter.

I nodded. 'I wish I'd gone with you to Tashco too, Jon. You knew I wanted to, more than anything. I just couldn't leave Stuart – then. Now I see what was going on, I just feel so awful.'

'Oh, my dear little Saskia,' he said, stroking my cheek.

'Jon, you know I'll do whatever you want.'

He leant over and began to kiss me then, a long, slow, non-brotherly kiss, as if we had all the time in the world to explore one another's bodies.

List of Things I Don't Want to be Doing When I'm Forty

1 Collecting Brillo pads.
2 Listening to my body clock.
3 Working as someone's assistant.
4 Still putting off starting a pension plan.
5 Saying 'I understand' when a man explains why he can't see me any more.
6 Renting my spare room to girls who have more luck with men than me.
7 Accepting my mother's judgement of me.
8 Drinking beer from the bottle.
9 Being involved with shows like *Experiences in White*.
10 Missing my date with destiny.

I didn't insist on going halves with the bill, reminding myself that it wasn't in the spirit of the new immorality to be uptight about things like that. Jon stuck it on his card, which I noticed was a Platinum – v. impressive, if slightly surprising. He mumbled something about an aunt dying and leaving him piles of money.

'Some people have all the aunts,' I told him, but spoilt the effect of my witticism by going on about my own aunt who lived in an old person's home in Kent and collected Brillo pads. She was especially fond of the blue ones, but I suspected that she'd leave those to Rebecca.

Unfortunately, we never did make it under the table that night and Jon drove me home straight after the coffee (and the story of my aunt). Even sadder was the fact that he didn't ask to come in, which was more than a bit deflating given the nature of his kisses. Like I said, lots of sex before thirty was imperative, given that I didn't envisage a lot of it taking place afterwards.

I dropped a little hint as we drove past Pharmacy restaurant, with all its medicine boxes in the window, declaring humorously that it looked like the sort of place where you could buy condoms. But Jon just curled the corner of his mouth in one of those wry smiles that men pushing forty start giving in order to avoid too many wrinkles forming around the mouth area.

Actually he grew all serious when he stopped the car. He cupped my face in his hands so that I felt like I was at the dentist's waiting for a filling. He reminded me of my promise to say nothing to anyone about Stuart's money-laundering, especially Stuart. I felt a bit stupid with my cheeks squeezed together, but I fluttered my eyelashes gamely in the hope of closing the sex deal. All I got was a peck on the forehead. V. maddening.

'Sleep well,' he muttered dispassionately as I dragged myself from the car in what I hoped was an inviting fashion, giving him a large expanse of leg from the slit in my silver knee-length pencil skirt. I'd nicked it from Rebecca years ago when showing expanses of my leg still drove men wild. But it wasn't working now.

Inside, Alice was lying stretched out on the stripped maple of our living-room floor. She was polishing up her shoe collection, which was strewn from one end of the flat to the other.

'So?' she said expectantly as soon as I walked in. She must have noticed my smeared lipstick. Always a dead give-away.

'So what?' I replied, all wide-eyed and wonderfully innocent.

'For starters, where did you two get to? What went on? Are you an item? Did he? Dish girl, dish!'

'Well, he snogged me in the gallery and then he took me to a restaurant in Clerkenwell and snogged me there as well,' I squealed excitedly, jumping up and down with unbelievable girlish glee.

'I knew it,' she cried, entering into the spirit of the thing. Throwing her shoe cloth in the air, I guess she was delighted with her powers as a clairvoyant. 'I knew it! Didn't I tell you he had the hots for you? He's so into you, Sass, I knew it. It had to happen. This is so great.'

'It is great, isn't it?'

'So, did you do it?'

'We were in a restaurant,' I told her primly.

'Oh, yeah, right, and you couldn't, like, dive under a table or into the loos, or something? What happened to the new immorality?' she asked, looking slightly mystified.

'We had some serious stuff to discuss,' I explained, starting to deflate again at my lack of powers to seduce Jon into going all the way.

'Yeah?' she conceded, vaguely going back to polishing a red-patent whore shoe with darling little love-heart buckles on the side. I sat down on the sofa and picked up its mate. Suddenly I felt like a total failure and began to give myself the 'Jon only loves you in a brotherly way' speech again.

After a bit, Alice looked up at me and grinned. 'Anyway I'm really pleased for you both; you were made for each other.'

I was still trying to get settled on our big chrome sofa, which was impossibly uncomfortable. This artist guy I'd dated once at college gave it to me as a parting gift after I caught him snogging my tutor. He was really famous for them now, or I would have chucked it out ages ago.

'You don't look too thrilled,' she said.

'It's just this sofa,' I lied.

'Oh,' she nodded. 'Yeah, that's why I always sit on the floor – it's better for your spine anyway apparently.'

'Anything's better for your spine than this monster,' I snapped. Why hadn't Jon wanted to come in and kiss me some more?

'Well, anyway, it's so great. I'm really, really pleased for you both. Do you want a drink to celebrate? You should have invited him in.'

'No, I think I'll stick to water,' I told her, ignoring the inviting him in issue.

'Good idea – think of your pores. Now that you're going

to be doing a lot of up close and personal, you need to watch these things.'

I started fidgeting with the pair of her red whore shoe, examining the startlingly high heel. 'Alice, you don't think he only loves me in a brotherly way, do you? I mean, we have known each other for, like, ever.'

'No, of course not. Besides, he snogged you, didn't he?'

'Well, yeah, but you don't, you know, what I mean is, you don't think he just snogged me in a brotherly way, do you?'

She threw the cloth at me. 'God, you're crazy. Where do you get these ideas? Brotherly snogging? Saskia!'

I began to feel better immediately, and agreed with her that we should have a drink to celebrate.

She jumped up, passing me the other shoe to finish polishing. 'I've got some vodka in the fridge. When are you seeing him next, anyway?'

'Um, well, that's the thing,' I told her, the doubts returning with a vengeance. I was acutely aware that our future hadn't been discussed in the kind of detail that a girl pushing thirty needs it to be discussed. I needed to inject a bit of happening muscle into my future, which had been suffering from a rather alarming droop lately. 'I don't know,' I shrugged. 'We had a lot of other things to talk about, see.'

'Oh, well,' Alice breezed, kicking her way through her shoe horde to the kitchen. 'I suppose you'll see him soon enough. The Saatchi opening's next week. You can go together.'

'Yeah,' I agreed, 'and the next week's my birthday.'

'But listen,' she called out from the kitchen. 'I haven't told you my news. Well, it's your news more than my news, really.'

'You've not decided to stick with Jim, have you?' I called out to her.

'No way. I'm going out with Matt now.'

'Oh,' I said, thinking of his T-cells. 'I suppose at least you've got a read-out of his genetic make-up.'

'I didn't say we were going to *breed*. But that's not my news. No, it's nothing to do with me. It's Piers, the American who bought that show from you.'

'Shit!' I cried, suddenly remembering. 'I had a date with him tonight. I forgot all about it.'

'Saskia, you dark horse! Haven't you got the boys throwing themselves at you now? And to think, it was only the other day that you swore you'd never have another boyfriend.'

'Oh fuck, fuck, *fuck*!'

'Exactly my point. He called around seven. Flowers, the whole deal. And it's official: he's even better-looking in real life. If you're really going to fall in love with Jon, I might go for Piers myself. I put the flowers in your bedroom, and they are not the guilt flowers you can pick up at Texaco, either. He seemed quite shattered to find you'd forgotten him.'

I groaned. 'What did you tell him?'

'I told him you had a business meeting.'

'Shit, shit, shit, shit, shit.'

'That's what he said.' She shook her head and smiled. You might want to give up lists and start a diary, now that you are so heavily in demand.'

My Best Assets

1   Ability to tell one bald head from another at crowded art shows.
2   Knowing which openings serve the best booze.
3   Encyclopaedic knowledge of London contemporary art scene, including addresses and star signs of all major players.
4   Faith in my hair's ability to endure further colourants.
5   Encyclopaedic knowledge of best places to buy vintage clothing.
6   Seven pairs of fifteen-denier tights (non bobbled).
7   My Wonderbra.
8   My legs – only they go a bit pear-shaped at the top (see also list entitled My Flaws).
9   GSOH. If you laugh the world laughs with you – or is that at you?
10 An individual style (see also list entitled My Flaws).
11 An eye for art and a bod for – well, whatever.
12 My stomach – pretty flat, especially when I avoid pizza for a week or more.
13 My friends.
14 My ability to bounce back.
15 The ability to appear far madder than I actually am.

I didn't see Jon all weekend. Nor for that matter did I see Piers, which didn't surprise me after I blew him out. He probably never wanted to see me again. Having gone from being dumped to being the dumper all in one evening was a shock.

Still, it was a bit of a boost to the old self-esteem, suddenly being in a position to blow out a man like Piers. Gosh.

Naturally I wriggled out of the Saturday night blind-date thing at Rebecca's. I mean, I had to be on hand for Jon, in case he wanted to whisk me off somewhere and make mad passionate love to me, natch.

Alice looked v. dubious at this justification.

I told Rebecca that I was counting the calories in my kitchen cupboard. This excuse struck her as satisfactory, as she considered calorie-counting to be right up there as one of the highest virtues on earth.

'Good idea,' she agreed. 'To tell you the truth, Saskia, I don't think Jeremy's friend Simon was right for you anyway. It's my hunch that he's looking for a girl with assets of her own, you see.'

Wasn't everyone?

I put the phone down and started making a list of my assets, but after a lot of pencil-chewing, I more or less lost interest. When a girl gets to the stage where she counts her knowledge of which gallery openings serve the best booze and fifteen-denier tights as her assets, it's time to give up.

I tried to get on to Sophie all weekend to share my news about Jon, but her answering machine was diverting calls to her mobile, and her mobile was switched off. Albert was busy helping Sal to move into his Bayswater flat.

Alice had gone over to Matt's studio on Saturday morning and I didn't expect to see her for the rest of the weekend. He was trying to convince her to have a DNA reading done, which involved her giving samples of her bodily fluids. He was especially keen on blood samples. The things girls do for love.

I wandered around the Portobello Road on Saturday and bought a vintage lace dress that felt as though it might dissolve on first wearing, but would definitely look brilliant with the orange hessian shoes. More or less. That's what the girl who owned the store said, anyway.

My planned revenge on Emmanuel had taken second place to my planned seduction of Jon now, but with this dress, I'd be killing two birds with one stone.

I spent the afternoon in the Lisboa café nibbling hard little Portuguese cakes. I was wearing sunglasses, Emmanuel's jeans and one of his tee shirts knotted at the front to reveal my navel ring. That was where I started jotting down my list of all the things I loved about Jon. All the little things took on a much greater significance now that I examined them as a prelude to our kiss.

We had been an item waiting to happen, I mused, chewing my bottom lip reflectively. I've always been a romantic, although given the choice between marriage and a two-week fling, I'll take the fling every time. Not that I don't want love to last for ever, it's just that I don't want to lose the intensity of those first shared intimacies.

And that was the odd thing about Jon and me getting together after all these years. We knew one another so well;

everything was already v. familiar. Just the same, I wrote the list and compared it favourably to a list I'd made ages ago about all the things I hated about Emmanuel.

Alice rang me on Saturday night and I practically broke my leg on the chrome sofa charging to grab the receiver. I was hoping it would be Jon, natch. She was ringing to ask whether I'd heard from him, and I felt thoroughly rejected and unlovable as I admitted that he hadn't called. I prattled on about how I'd been out all day and he had probably been ringing non-stop.

'Wasn't the answering machine on?' She asked rather obviously, but I breezed over that detail, muttering about how boring it is waiting for the beeps and that Jon was a man of the moment, and how he was probably on his mobile going through a hugely long tunnel.

Alice interrupted me and said she had to go. She sounded a bit uncomfortable actually, and I envisaged Matt siphoning off her blood products for his DNA works of art.

I spent Saturday evening doing my nails and conditioning my hair and watching a movie about The Beatles' early years in Hamburg, when Stu Sutcliffe fell in love with Astrid. When it was over, I dug up my list of hairstyles I'd like to try and added Blonde Mop, deciding that a blonde mop was just what I needed post-thirty to make me feel young and hip and desirable.

It didn't look that hard to do, and before the night was out I had a go at cutting it myself, using a stainless steel salad bowl to keep my scissors even. When I took the bowl off it was obvious that my aim had gone badly wrong, especially round the back. I looked like a friendless German tourist on the hunt for Carnaby Street.

Now I would have to make up a story about how it happened. I thought I might say that I fell asleep chewing gum, which had actually happened to me once, and with my excuse at the ready I began to feel better for a moment before

I realised that the story wouldn't satisfy Albert for a second. Once he saw what I'd done to my hair he'd hit the roof. Or me even!

I fell asleep writing a v. extensive list of people who may have Saskia Williams on their hit list.

On Sunday I spent the morning turning all the mirrors in the flat around so that I wouldn't have to look at myself. The mirror in the bathroom was stuck to the wall, so I smeared it all over with soap. Then I wrapped my head in an old scarf with images of Parisian tourist sites all over it and went out to buy the Sunday papers. Jake was sitting at one of the outdoor cafés I passed on the way.

'Hey, Saskia, cut your hair again?' he taunted as I walked by grandly with my tartan shopping trolley (had to lug all those Sunday papers back in something).

I adhered strictly to my list of foods I must avoid and subsisted on fruit and water till midday, when I busted and binged out on cornflakes and stale crumpets with jam.

Feeling a bit better in the afternoon, I added Having Sex with Jon to my list of all the things I wanted to do before I turned thirty.

Things a Girl must Never Do during Early Courtship

1 Stay home on Saturday night on the off chance.
2 Say 'I love you' first.
3 Cook, clean or wash his socks for him.
4 Cut your hair or change your appearance in any way.
5 Let him see you in your nightie.
6 Take him seriously when he says he finds your nightie 'cute'.
7 Introduce him to your mother.
8 Tell him how long it is since you've had sex.
9 Turn to him for help.

I was slightly late for work on Monday because I fell asleep Sunday night with a cucumber mask on my face. It took forever to get off when I woke up.

I was hoping that a glowing complexion would distract attention from my absurd hairstyle. But the instructions on the mask said to leave on for five minutes, and I'd gone nine hours over time. V. bad news.

When I did manage to scrub it off, my skin was so red that I was afraid of inadvertently stopping traffic on the way to work. I stuck on my Jackie O. glasses in the hope of minimising my impact, and opted for this gorgeous long black thing which I bought at Portobello from a bloke who said he was a retired priest.

He had told me that he used to wear it under his vestments for funeral services, which sounded a bit dodgy hygiene-wise. Anyway it was long and tight, with a fab little line of buttons all the way down to the ground. Nehru collar, natch. I looked quite the young monk. A Franciscan monk, given the haircut, although I spiked that up and tried to make it look intentional.

On my way down to the tube Jake called out some very non-confidence-boosting insults about Rasputin but I managed to ignore him. I wasn't going to let anyone bring me down today, I told myself. In fact, such was my mood that I said all sorts of positive self-esteem-raising things to myself on my journey, which paid off because a nervous-looking bloke in a suit gave me his seat – mistaking my mutterings for those of a wandering madwoman who lived for the joy of knifing men like him in the groin.

Walking out of the tube station on Bond Street, my positivity took a bit of a dip. The sun, which had shone all weekend, had left town and it looked like a midwinter's day. In the Jackie O. sunglasses I could hardly see a thing.

When I arrived at A SPACE I went from beetroot red to purple and then to white. I even tried to hyperventilate, but I had enough trouble just kick-starting my lungs to work. I gasped once loudly and then waited for total collapse.

The door to the gallery was open and the entire *Experiences in White* show was gone. I began to shake as I remembered running out of the gallery on Friday after the phone call, and realised that I couldn't have locked up.

As I walked into the space, things appeared to be worse than even my overactive imagination could have guessed.

The glass desk in the middle of the space was cleft in two, as if one of those kung fu champs had been in throwing the sides of his hands around. I called out to Stuart, and as my echo bounced around the empty walls, a niggling voice told me that I was in deep shit.

Let's face it, I hadn't exactly been focused on security when I fled work after the mystery caller, and since then I hadn't been focused on much at all – apart from my libido, natch. But surely Stuart would have popped in after his dodgy dealings at the auction? Surely the gallery wasn't open all weekend? Surely we were insured?

My list of surelys was cut short when a closer inspection of the gallery revealed that the storeroom had been ransacked as well, and anything of value taken. Files were strewn all over the place. In fact, the only part of the gallery still intact was the kitchenette. Whoever looted A SPACE clearly had brain enough to leave the Chardonnay to others.

As I was examining the kitchenette, I heard footsteps in the gallery and even knowing that it was probably Stuart coming back to perform a ritual killing on me cheered me up. Being alone was starting to make me feel a bit creepy.

'Hello?' I called out, praying to a God I didn't believe in that it wasn't the kung fu guy out for another attack. I didn't think I could defend myself very well in this tight priest's undervest, or whatever it was.

But it wasn't Stuart.

'Hello!' two unfamiliar male voices called back.

They walked in just as I was taking the bottle of Chardonnay out to use as a weapon.

Two plain-clothes policemen introduced themselves, shoving a couple of badges under my face. There was an older one and a younger one, a sort of cool-cop, old-cop duo. Checking out the bottle in my hand, the younger of the two grinned. 'Busted!' he said.

'What?' I squealed. V. paranoid obviously.

'Busted,' announced my interlocutor blankly. He pointed to the bottle.

'You mean this?' I said with a brevity I didn't feel. 'Do you want a drink?'

The older detective raised an eyebrow.

'Just joking,' I laughed, sticking it back in the fridge.

'You go ahead, though,' the younger one said. 'We won't judge you.'

No, I thought to myself, you'll leave that to the jury.

They asked for Stuart and seemed satisfied when I said that I didn't know when he'd be in. I started to exhale, imagining that they'd take their leave and busy themselves with a spot of clamping. No such luck.

'Bit of damage to the table over here,' the younger one remarked, pointing to what was left of the triangular glass desk. The older one nodded. There were papers strewn amid the debris and in a flood of horror, I recognised them as my bored doodles, the wretched lists I made to amuse myself through the hours of painful nothingness which Stuart inflicted on me.

'You mean the glass debris? That's a work of art. A highly respected Russian deconstructivist,' I blurted. 'We were very fortunate to get him.'

'Get him?' the older detective repeated as if there was something suspicious in the term.

'Of course, he's very much in demand,' I explained in my haughtiest Bond Street dealer voice.

'Yeah, I can see why,' said the younger detective derisively as he crouched down and began riffling through my papers on the floor.

'Yes; more or less the man of the era,' I lied.

'Is he?' the older detective replied, raising his eyebrows as if he didn't believe a word of it. That's what I hate about the police, they're so suspicious. 'What's his name, then, this Russian deconstructivist?'

'Sorry?' I said, distracted by the intensity with which the younger detective was now studying one of the pages he had picked up.

'His name?'

'Oh, yes, Boris um er Boris Bernsteinavich. Yes, that's it.'

He nodded as if he was trying to match the name to a face on *Crime Stoppers*. 'Get a lot for a piece like that then, do you?'

'Sure I can't offer you a drink?' I blurted as the younger detective stood up, studying one of my pages v. intensely, as if he was expecting to sit a test on it later. I was trying to make out which list it was. I mean, it could be anything, I was always jotting things down.

He'd probably come across my list of foods I was going to live on and mistaken it for a list of illegal substances. Wheatgrass might sound v. suspicious to a guy who wears a Marks & Spencer's suit for a living. I peered at the page, trying to decipher a key word, but my sunglasses were a bit smudged after my tube journey.

On second thoughts I decided that it looked like my list of men I planned to sleep with before I turned thirty – probably checking to see if he was on it. They have v. huge egos, these young detectives.

'We have Chardonnay,' I added for no reason at all except perhaps to show them how odd I was and make them want to leave. I'd seen that device used on *The Bill*. Criminals confuse the police with aberrant behaviour until they eventually do the cops' heads in and one cop says to the other cop, 'Let's go and see if anyone has died in police custody while we were out, shall we, Constable?'

The older detective informed me that it was only ten-thirty in the morning, and the way he looked at me as he said it suggested that he had me down as a crazed alcoholic. No doubt he thought that the glasses were concealing the bloodshot eyes of the dipsomaniac, and I dare say my red face wasn't helping my case any more than the cassock thing.

'What's this then?' the young detective asked, finally passing over the page he'd been studying. The words I read made me feel nauseous.

LIST OF ALL THE PEOPLE I WANT TO SEE DEAD was written in capitals.

Heading the list was Stuart Dumass – natch. As I scanned the dog-eared list, his name seemed to jump out at me all over the place.

V. v. bad news.

I laughed nervously, and then as I realised they weren't seeing the joke, I upped the ante a bit and bent over at the waist with belly laughter. Laugh and the world laughs with you, etc.

'Oh, my *hit list*,' I chuckled, holding my sides for effect. 'It's all part of the new immorality, you see. I mean, it's nothing serious, obviously; everyone's on it,' I breezed. 'It's not an exclusive list at all.'

'Really?' said the older detective, taking the list from me and scanning it. 'And this new immorality, what exactly is it? A cult or something?'

I started to laugh again but stopped after a bit because the boys in M&S suits weren't really looking like they were much in the mood for humour at this time of the morning. Not while they were on duty, anyway.

'Yes, well, it's more of a philosophy, really, a sort of "whatever turns you on" attitude to ethics.' I shrugged my shoulders and grinned my sweetest grin.

The detectives exchanged a look that seemed to suggest they didn't think a 'whatever turns you on' attitude to ethics was a v. sound idea.

I assured them that it was, rattling off words like sophisticated and post-moralist and, well, a lot of rubbish mostly, till they appeared to grow weary of me and moved back to the subject of Stuart.

They asked me where he'd gone and at what time he'd left and when I was expecting him back or if I was. I thought the last bit rather cheeky.

I told them he'd popped out for some loo rolls and would enter the purchase in the list of gallery events the moment he walked in.

'Very good,' said the older detective. 'When might that be?'

I asked him how long was a piece of string, but I could see I'd rubbed them up the wrong way over the 'whatever' attitude to ethics remark and so I reassured them I would let Stuart know they'd dropped in and told them to have a nice day.

God, was I relieved when they left – I half expected the older one to tell me not to make plans for leaving town. Naturally I got straight onto the phone to Jon, who told me to meet him at his flat.

I locked up, v. carefully this time, and tore down to the tube.

Things I must Not Do in front of the Man I Love

1   Nab the last bit of food on his plate in a restaurant.
2   Shove my grey knickers in my bra to make my tits look bigger.
3   Housework (don't want to give him ideas).
4   Look at other men while nudging him in the ribs and winking.
5   Sleep with my mouth open.
6   Shop (are you kidding, *me* rummaging through the £5 piles on Portobello? Even I would run).
7   Allow him to see my lists (natch).
8   Talk after sex.

He started kissing my neck greedily as soon as he opened the door of his loft apartment. Then he worked his way down my chest, pulling open the thousands of buttons running down my dress and skilfully removing my bra (such as it was).

By the time he got to my lower abdomen it was all I could do to cry out something deeply uncool like, 'Don't stop! Don't stop!' or 'Do it to me, baby!' like some B-grade porn star. Thoughts of the police and breaking and entering were replaced by thoughts of 'Will he have to stop doing these amazing things to my body to get his condom?' The answer came almost straight away.

'I've got to go and get a condom.'

At the point of reckoning I was spreadeagled across his entrance hall. I really didn't want to move. Really not. He was snogging me against a spectacular wall of granite, cold, hard and v.divine. Once he pulled me away from it I felt like I was on fire.

He led me into his bedroom and while he went to the drawer for a condom, I made a mental note to add the wall of Jon's flat to my list of best places to make love.

As a lover, Jon was more your pillaging army rather than skilled surgeon. I've had both and I prefer the pillagers. Emmanuel was very much the skilled surgeon, delivering my orgasm like it was a baby. Sometimes he even said, 'Come on, baby, you can do it!' like a gynaecologist coaxing an exhausted mother to breathe through the final stages of labour.

Even as Jon's pillaging army swarmed through my body, I couldn't stop uneasy thoughts popping into my consciousness V. disconcerting. The most pressing concern was what had happened to Stuart. I couldn't stop imagining him strung up to a drip somewhere. My mother is always telling me I'll hurt myself on my imagination one day. And I did, just as Jon discovered my G-spot.

When we made love the second time I grew pensive about the girl I'd seen Jon with that night at Cantaloupe, and lost my flow. Not wanting to disappoint Jon, I still told him I'd come.

Something wasn't right, and all the orgasms in the world (fake or otherwise) weren't going to help. I guess at the end of the day I needed more than sex to distract me from my worries.

I did come eventually, though. We made love five times in all, and even I'm not that competent an actress. Each time Jon was more aggressive than the last, we had sex in every position in every place in the loft. We ended up back in bed, utterly spent.

And then the nagging doubts and worries started up again. There was no doubt about it – and I'm not complaining, really I'm not – but we still had stuff that needed dealing with. Like where the hell was Stuart, for one?

But I got the impression from the way Jon was virtually passed out across my body that this was not the time for talking. I usually find that most of the talking in a relationship is done before the sex bit. If you have something you want to say to a man, say it while he's still desperate for your body because once the sex is over, he won't want to be bothered.

I don't know why that should be, but it is. After sex, women are much chattier than men. Men don't feel like saying anything more complicated than 'Wow!' Or, 'Wasn't that great?' I think the word is mellow, and men like to enjoy their after-sex mellowness in silence.

Men want to kick back after sex while the other person makes coffee or proposes cigarettes. I know because I've had many a post-coital argument over who the other person should be. I don't see why it has to be me.

Jon opened his eyes as I was thinking this stuff, and proposed coffee. I agreed to milk and nine sugars and he went right off and made it, which sorted out that little worry at least.

I kicked back and admired his view. It was three in the afternoon and I felt like a different woman to the girl who'd frantically knocked on Jon's door all those hours ago. Amazing what sex can do for tension – those biochemists want to get to work on that one. Make a little pill that mimics the effects of the post-sexual glow.

If I could just deal with these last few remaining doubts about Stuart's safety, the likelihood of my arrest for murder and who Jon was snogging in Cantaloupe the other night, I'd feel perfectly relaxed. I rummaged in my bag for a pen and pad and started a list of concerns that were prohibiting me from discovering my true bliss.

Jon's loft was above his gallery looking out over the spires and council flats of east London, and I wondered why I'd never been invited before. Actually no one I knew had ever been invited to Jon's loft. For a gregarious party-till-you-drop kind of guy he lived a very private life. Which is what made him so insanely sexy.

He had owned the loft for a few years and spent close to a fortune doing it up. I knew that because he'd been in a real state over money once or twice at A SPACE towards the end. Now I could see why. There was an entire wall of glass that made London look like a *trompe l'oeil*.

Jon returned with the coffees and we drank them looking

out over London. He stood behind me and periodically nibbled at my ear. Despite the morning's events, I couldn't help feeling utterly blissful and serene within my body, at least.

They say that a woman in her thirties is more sexually tuned in than her youthful sisters, and more likely to have multiple orgasms and discover G-spots, which is cruel given that she's far less likely to have sex.

Jon had moved on from my ears to my neck and I started to feel turned on again. But the feelings I was beginning to have for Jon were a million times deeper than sex. This could even be love. Maybe I'd always loved him. I wondered all these things and more as Jon sent shivers through my body, and wished there was a switch I could flick to turn my brain off.

I had to know if the same thoughts were going through Jon's head. Why had we put off this magnificent event for so long? Why had we waited?

I quite simply couldn't stop myself, and yet as the words fell clumsily out of my mouth, I knew I'd misjudged the situation – like I always do. I turned around and looked up into his eyes and wondered if it wasn't too late to change the subject or to make a joke, even.

Jon looked down at me with those lovely dark eyes of his, and just as I was about to tell him the one about the Frenchman who goes into a bar with a dog and an elephant, he folded me into his arms and held me against his heart.

'Isn't it enough that we're here now?' he whispered.

And if I'd have been honest I would have said, 'Actually no, it's not.'

But I was almost thirty: I'd learnt from bitter experience that speaking my mind wasn't always in my best interests. As it was, I was saved further embarrassment by the phone ringing in the other room. Jon kissed the top of my head and wandered off. He said as he left that he wouldn't be a minute but he was gone for ages.

Left alone, I did what any girl does in a new lover's pad and began to browse. Well, it's a natural drive, and down on my list of things a girl should do on a date. Open the sock drawer – v. telling.

In this case the wardrobe was even more of an eye-opener than I expected. Wow! The way Jon arranged his clothing was positively fascist – talk about ordered. Everything was aligned and organised, not a cuff poking out. I could imagine his trousers goose-stepping into their creases.

Each shirt was neatly hung beside rows of other shirts – no cross-dressing in this wardrobe. He probably had border-control checks to keep rogue jackets getting in among the shirts and running amok. The only word for it was – *fuck*!

Trying to measure this propensity for order against the abandoned passion of his lovemaking made me quite dizzy. I was finding this man v. troubling. There were no pictures or ornaments that might give him away, no clues as to the real Jon, not even any hint of the Jon I'd known for years – or thought I had.

It was clinical, that's what it was; cold and impersonal. But v. cool and hip, natch. Just like all those loft pads in the Sunday papers that Alice and I liked to laugh about and say stuff about, like, 'Oh, right, and we're meant to believe that people actually live like that? A life devoid of cornflakes on the counter and yesterday's clothes strewn across the sofa? As if.'

But here was the living proof. Jon would probably die if I left my smelly clothes over his sofa for the night. He'd probably stick his wardrobe commandant onto me.

I told myself that ornaments and mess were passé. Dis-organisation holds you down. I read that in *Businesswoman Weekly*. Actually the thought of being held down by Jon Tashco quite thrilled me.

Jon came back into the room and began to dress. 'I have to go,' he said blandly, as he tidied up the mess my eyes had made while roaming his wardrobe earlier. I made a ridiculous excuse about looking for my favourite shirt, but he ignored me, closing the cupboard with a thud.

'Are you going to be all right if I drop you back at the gallery?' he asked. 'Or do you want to stay with Alice?'

'No: I really should face the music with Stuart,' I sighed, not feeling a bit like doing any such thing. 'I mean, that is, if he's back.'

'Don't worry about Stuart. He can take care of himself. Don't forget what I told you though. Say *nothing*.'

I was getting a bit sick of him telling me this but I nodded agreeably, flashing him one of my cute and adorable looks. He set about lacing up his shoes. 'I'll need to leave soon,' he said while I was still rummaging through the bedclothes for my underwear.

'Keeping your mouth shut is going to be even more important now that he's got the police after him. If they're onto him, you want to stay well out of it.'

'But surely they don't actually want to arrest him, do they?' I asked as I discovered my tights in a ball with my knickers and bra. 'How do you know they want to arrest him. They might just have been patrolling the neighbourhood, checking locks.'

Jon groaned.

'No, seriously,' I insisted. 'Maybe someone reported the break-in? They didn't mention wanting to arrest him. At least, I don't think they did. No, they didn't, I'm sure of it. They were quite nice, really – even asked about the Russian deconstructivist that we're showing.'

'What Russian deconstructivist? I thought you were showing that Hewit idiot.'

I decided not to pursue the fictional Boris saga, but I was damned if I was going to have Hewit knocked after I'd managed to sell the whole show. 'Hang on a minute, I sold that whole show.'

'Sorry, I shouldn't have said that. But it stands to reason, doesn't it? I mean, after everything Albert told you. They must be onto him. Come on, Saskia, Stuart's in this thing up to his eyeballs.'

I struggled with the clip on my bra. 'You know that's what I find so strange. Stuart comes across so straight. I just can't see him at the centre of a large-scale fraud.'

'Maybe you don't know Stuart as well as you think,' he said, sounding a touch irritated with me.

Maybe he was right; I probably didn't know Stuart. I was still worried about him, though. I was worried about where he was and whether he was all right. It was a habit with me, I explained to Jon as I tried to share my concerns. 'I can't help worrying about where he is.'

'Believe me, he's lying low. And so should you.'

Jon dropped me at A SPACE and once again left without saying when we might meet again. It was only after I saw him disappear that I realised I didn't have a key and wouldn't be able to get in. But when I tried the door it opened, yet I was certain I'd locked up before I left. I called out, but no one answered.

List of Things I should Get Professional Help to Sort

1 My belief that men who don't want to sleep with me want to chop me up into small pieces.
2 My belief in public transport as survival nightmare. Sometimes I can't sit in an underground carriage without wondering what my fellow passengers would taste like if I had to eat them in an emergency, or something.
3 My fear that if I don't orgasm with a man during sex he'll be insulted and toss me away like a used condom.
4 My wardrobe.
5 Fear of women with matching accessories, eg matching shoes and handbag.
6 My compulsive list-making.
7 My use of knickers as bra-padders. I'm not sure or anything but this could be v. sicko behaviour; I mean, I've never seen Ally McBeal do it.

'Stuart arranged delivery this morning. Took me by surprise,' Piers explained. 'They're here at the office now – which is odd, given the last time I spoke to him he insisted that the show wasn't coming down until the end of the month. Funny guy, your boss.'

I exhaled loudly. So Stuart *was* alive. 'But you have the paintings now, so everything's OK?' I confirmed.

'I have them here in the reception of my building,' he repeated. 'I'll, er, be exhibiting them with the rest of the collection, naturally,' he explained nervously. 'Why wouldn't everything be OK?'

'Just checking, that's all. Part of the A SPACE service,' I trilled.

He didn't respond, which I took to mean he thought I was barking. But I didn't care: at least a bandit hadn't legged it with my big sale; at least Stuart was alive.

I don't think I could have coped if anything had happened to those paintings. I mean, I'd virtually earned my yearly salary in commission on this sale, which I know sounds really shallow and base, but as a girl about to enter the realm of ultimate adulthood, I had to take stock of my assets.

In fact, apart from my fifteen-denier tights and an awesome understanding of the London underground, this commission was my only *real* asset. My nest egg, yes, that's what it was. Heck, I could finally start a pension plan with this. My mother would be pleased. That's if I didn't blow it on a weekend of Bacchanalian excess in the Big Apple. Which, thinking about it, seemed a much better way to spend it.

'So is everything OK with you?' Piers enquired, probably envisaging me counting my thimble collection on the desk.

'Yup,' I told him. 'Fine and dandy.' He didn't sound convinced, but I told him I had a customer and had to go.

Fine and dandy? I rolled the absurd phrase around my mind after I hung up and realised that it was true: everything was just peachy. Piers had his paintings, Stuart was alive and I was in love with Jon. So while I was probably up for a bloody big neck-wringing for leaving the gallery unlocked over the weekend, I was at least out of the woods as far as murder charges went. Phew.

No doubt Stuart would probably want body parts as compensation for the loss of his desk, but I could deal with all that now that I had found true love. Stuart had quite rightly seen the sense of clearing the gallery of the *Experiences in White* show in the event of spraying it with my blood. Stuart was practical even where crimes of passion were concerned.

The only cloud in my life's sky was Piers's tone, which I found v. odd. He hadn't even mentioned our date or lack thereof and thinking about it, he had seemed a tad cagey. I mean, he can't have been looking forward to his date with me all that much not to have worried about where I'd disappeared to. Not that I cared too deeply, obviously not. Not now that I was involved with Jon. Course I didn't.

Following the phone call and a bit of idle time-wasting, I went about cleaning up the gallery as best I could. I started by sweeping up the glass shards which were spread over a large expanse of the exhibition space. No doubt insurance would cover the desk, but I couldn't see Stuart finding it in his heart to hand over curatorial responsibility to a girl who'd breezed out of the gallery on Friday afternoon without so much as bothering to put the door on the latch, let alone set the alarm.

Especially now the police were after him.

'I didn't hear you,' Stuart said, suddenly appearing from the stairs of the storeroom.

It was all I could do to stay upright. 'I didn't know you were here either,' I whispered, my voice slightly choked. 'I was just, er, just clearing up the glass, as you can see.'

'Leave it,' he said gently. 'The cleaners are coming in this evening. I should have phoned you, told you not to come in, but I was distracted.'

He was standing a fair distance away. We were speaking from across a gulf, and as his voice echoed around me I felt strangely calmed. 'You OK?' he asked.

'Yes, I am,' I nodded meekly. 'I'm sorry about the table.'

'Yes,' he agreed, still standing on the other side of the gallery, our words bouncing around the walls.

'Were you insured?'

'Yes, I was. Thank you.'

I felt like we were foreigners in a classroom, learning to speak conversational English. 'Well, that's one thing then.'

'Yes.'

I wondered if I should enquire as to when he had my homicide pencilled in so that I could plan my evening. It was around five-thirty, and I was normally making noises about wanting to get back to my life by this time on a Monday.

Stuart must have sensed my mood. 'You can go if you want.'

'Thank you,' I said as I walked over towards the far corner and started gathering up my bag. He watched me without moving from his post, which made me feel v. paranoid.

'Saskia,' he called just as I put my hand on the door.

I spun around. He looked so diminutive, standing there in the vast expanse of empty space. I felt like I was looking down the wrong end of a telescope. He seemed unsure and concerned. Not a bit villainish. 'Yes?' I replied.

'I was just going to say that I delivered the paintings to Dexter. I mean, if you were worried.'

'Thank you.' I waited, unsure whether he'd finished what he wanted to tell me. And it wasn't till I turned to open the door again that he spoke.

'Only I know you were planning on spending the commission on a holiday, so I'll forward the money straight to your account.'

'Yes.'

'If that's OK with you,' he added.

'That's great,' I said numbly, knowing there were so many other things I should have said. But not now, not here with twenty metres of empty space between us. Not when there were already so many more pressing things that we'd avoided discussing. Things about Jon, and auctions and money-laundering.

I hadn't even told him about the police.

'And Saskia, by the way. I love the hair.'

I put my hand to my rather odd haircut and smiled. 'Thanks.'

'You're looking good. The outfit, the glasses. It really suits you. But I'd better let you go, you'll have things to do. I'm not opening the gallery till the next show goes up. Give me a chance to clean up everything, you know?'

I nodded.

'The next show goes up the day after the Saatchi party. Perhaps I'll see you there?'

I nodded again. I couldn't speak. All I could think about was that Jon hadn't noticed my hair.

Things I Hate about My Boss – Abridged Version, Natch

1 The way he's really anal about organisation.
2 The way he looks at me as if I don't have a clue what's going on.
3 The way he does passive-aggressive stuff like giving me the afternoon off or lunch breaks as a way of making me feel useless.
4 The way he completely collapsed when Jon left – leaving me to pick up the pieces.
5 The way he didn't confront Jon or even seek revenge.
6 The way he doesn't smoke, drink or lose control.
7 The way he doesn't confide in me – v. distressing.

'What you should do is make a list,' Albert suggested calmly, completely ignoring the look of shock in my eyes. But this was classic Albert, so I don't know why I was surprised.

Sal was massaging conditioner into my hair. The haircut didn't look too bad now that I'd had my roots tinted, and Albert had been remarkably good about my foray into cutting.

I'd been telling them about how I couldn't believe that Stuart was all evil. Especially since he'd put the money in my account last week, and even suggested that I might like to put together a proposal for a show. When I revealed that he'd even gone so far as to recommend that I check out fares for tickets to New York, Sal and Albert exchanged significant looks.

It was now only a week before my birthday and despite a rather dodgy moment with the Emmanuel fiasco, I wasn't feeling nearly as hopeless as I had been. It was actually beginning to look as if my list of Things I must Achieve by Age Thirty was not a total write-off. Not that I was planning on following Albert's advice on lists again – natch. I promised him that hell would freeze over before I wrote another list on his say-so.

I even said I'd write that promise in blood for him if he wanted.

'No, listen. Honestly, it's a good idea, see. What you do is write down all Stuart's good qualities on one side of the page, and all Stuart's bad qualities on the other side, and then we'll have a look and see if it's the profile of a criminal.'

'No way,' I said in my when-hell-freezes-over voice. 'Besides, I can't think of any good things to say about him,' I lied. 'I just don't think he's really a criminal. After all, those police people didn't return.'

My argument was ignored, as another customer walked in. She was about seven feet tall in heels with a bowl of white curls on her head. She was the sort of girl that made other girls realise how pointless Wonderbras were.

'Hiya,' she said in one of those transatlantic, trans-pigeon-hole voices that prohibits you from placing someone and compartmentalising them as a *type*. V. annoying.

Albert moaned as if he was about to come in his pants. 'Evelyn *∂ah*-ling! My favourite client. You get more ravishing by the day.'

Somehow or other he had managed to get a cigarette in both hands, and was now waving the two of them around like an excited kid with a pair of sparklers on bonfire night.

Evelyn seemed to find this funny. I sat there po-faced, natch.

He was always doing that with cigarettes – forgetting that he had one alight and lighting up another. That's why he always kept a glass of champagne on hand. That way at least one hand was occupied with something other than smoking.

'Let me get you some champagne,' he sang. 'I've got a—'

But the girl didn't let him finish his sentence. She finished it for him. 'Special bottle of Moët just for me. Albert, you're perfect but I'm going to say no. I've got a submission to get in this afternoon and the bitch of a judge I'm before will bollock me if she gets a whiff of alcohol on my breath.'

She was air-kissing Sal as she said this, and I noticed that Sal lingered a bit long on the cheek-to-lip bit and not nearly long enough on the air bit. She sat down beside me and introduced herself. 'I know who you are,' she giggled. 'Albert doesn't stop talking about you. Saskia, right? Saskia of the new immorality lists fame?'

'Well I wouldn't be quite so famous for my lists if Albert didn't keep making me write them.' I poked my tongue out at him in the mirror. He rolled his eyes dramatically.

'She thinks the list I made her write about what she wants from a relationship made her last boyfriend dump her.'

'He was probably a bore anyway, am I right?' she asked. I shrugged.

She winked at Albert and rustled her curls prettily. 'Never put anything down in writing,' she whispered to me conspiratorially. 'And most of all, never sign anything that's been put in front of you by a man.'

Albert put his hands on his hips. 'I heard that, Ms Hornton, and I think I'll frazzle your roots for such disloyalty to my noble sex.'

Sal winked at her, and much to my chagrin I realised that somewhere in the last few minutes he had abandoned my scalp and was tenderly rubbing her shoulders.

She turned to me and smiled. Actually she was hard not to like, even if she was a size ten and gorgeous. 'I've heard a lot about your new immorality from Sal and Albert, and I must say I'm intrigued. I've got a big problem with morality myself.'

Albert snorted. 'You've got a problem finding out the meaning of the word, darling.'

Evelyn shot him a dirty look and then winked. 'It's a Catholic thing according to my therapist, but I wonder if it isn't a *girl* thing. No matter how hard I try I always find my morality chucking me into the arms of the most inappropriate men.'

'Lucky you,' I said. 'The only chucking I experience is men chucking me over.'

'Emmanuel was nothing but a common or garden French pig,' Albert tutted, pulling a comb through my hair.

I didn't want to tell him the truth, that I didn't care two pins for Emmanuel. Actually I was talking about Jon. The bastard hadn't called me since the sex, and Alice wasn't being v. supportive at all. She said he'd hardly been into the gallery since the day I'd seen him at his flat. But I got the feeling she was hiding something. She knew something, and wasn't telling.

'As soon as one bastard moves on, there's always another to take their place,' Evelyn sighed as if she'd done her thesis on it. 'And anyway, he probably only chucked you because he knew he was about to be chucked,' she assured me.

'Yes, I think that's it,' I agreed, feeling miles better. 'He knew I was going to chuck him, so he got in first.' I really, really liked this girl. She was a girl's girl after all.

'Now her boss is involved in a cash-for-questions scandal and money-laundering conspiracy,' Albert explained.

'It's only a scandal because you keep telling everyone about it,' I snapped.

Albert threw his hands in the air, both cigarettes burning away. 'Well, a boy's got to keep his customers amused, doesn't he? You don't think they come just for my scissors, do you?'

Evelyn and Sal giggled.

'Speaking of which, missy here took to her own hair the other week. Trying to replace my mastery with a salad bowl, would you believe?'

'I like it,' remarked Evelyn.

'That's not the point,' Albert said primly. 'It's my hair and I don't like my customers touching it.'

Evelyn laughed. 'Don't worry, Saskia, I've cut my own hair more than once. With dire results, I might add – actually you've done rather a good job. Maybe you should go into business.'

'Enough, Miss Hornton, or I'll hit you with my comb.'

Evelyn laughed. 'You work in an art gallery, don't you?' I nodded. 'Do you know, I've always found art *sooooo* intimidating,' she said. 'I think you are so brave.'

But I wasn't. Not a bit.

How to Spot that You're About to be Dropped

1   He doesn't call.
2   He doesn't return your calls when you call to find out why he hasn't called.
3   He turns up unexpectedly for sex.
4   Worse – he doesn't turn up unexpectedly for sex.
5   He doesn't turn up to a prearranged rendezvous.
6   Worse, he does turn up, but with another woman.
7   The other woman turns out to be your best friend.
8   He says it's purely platonic, but stops returning your calls.
9   Worse, so does she.

'Oh, my God, will you look at that?' Alice prompted, giving me a sharp jab in the ribs.

'Ouch! Don't always do that!'

'Well, look, will you. It's Jerry Hall talking to Elton John.'

I made the appropriate noises of amazement and delight and agreed with her that it was good to see the stars enjoying themselves.

Alice loved spotting the A-list, but whereas I liked to pretend that I didn't care, Alice cultivated no such pretensions. She would happily go ga-ga. I was with her once when she skated up to David Hockney in her blades and asked to stroke his dogs. V. embarrassing.

We were finally at the long-awaited Saatchi opening, where a collection of newly acquired American artists was being showcased with much fanfare and social networking.

Tons of famous people and people who looked like famous people were there. There were even famous people trying to look like they weren't a bit famous, swanning around as if recognition didn't matter to them in the least. As if.

But that's how seriously hot it was.

David Bowie, looking dapper in black, was chatting to Charles Saatchi in pinstripe. Mick Jagger was talking to one of the American artists – I couldn't remember her name but Emmanuel was always going on about how sexy she was, and how she was number one on his Women He'd Most Like to Sleep With list. I don't suppose I even got a mention.

Damien Hirst was bouncing around talking to Jay Joplin, but I hardly even smiled when he waved – I was too busy craning my neck for Jon, natch. The noise of a thousand people sipping wine, shovelling canapés down their throats and schmoozing one another was practically deafening, but I'd been to these things before and taken the precaution of wearing ear plugs.

The yellow lumps sticking out of my ears were v. embarrassing, admittedly, but then I was planning on whipping them out on spotting Jon.

Alice jabbed me again just as I was getting my body in position to lift a few olives to my mouth. I was finding it v. tricky to move, on account of the fact that every time I breathed out, the fragile antique lace of my dress tore a little more.

Vintage clothing is a lifestyle in itself. It's a bit like an elderly aunt who doesn't accept that you might have a life of your own. This dress thought I should be content to spend my time folding it up with mothballs.

This dress saw my wanting to wear it as the height of impertinence. As it was, I had to forgo dinner to avoid the risk of splitting a seam. And now, even above the roar of the art crowd, even with my ear plugs in place, I could hear my stomach rumbling – screaming for its supper.

The opening was already in full swing, which was just how we liked it normally, but this time I had another agenda (apart from keeping this dress on my back), and that was to notice and be noticed. For that you need a certain amount of space around you.

There was no space here; even the exhibits were fighting for their rights. People were getting v. annoyed by how much room the works of art were taking up. 'Most inconsiderate of Charles,' we heard a woman shriek when her hair got caught in a drip apparatus. 'Leaving all this art paraphernalia about is most inconsiderate of Charles.'

Art has always been a risky business.

It was cheek by jowl stuff. It was a struggle just getting a glass to your lips without knocking someone's eye out. When I did eventually work out who Alice was pointing at, I'd finally just managed to jam the olives in my mouth. I recognised the distinctive hairlines of Piers Dexter and Stuart and swallowed all three without chewing. For some reason, I'd presumed that Stuart would have been taken into police custody by now.

I stood on my vintage-shod toes to get a better look. It was definitely Stuart and Piers. They were both looking v. intense, and Alice put my worst fears into words by wondering out loud if Piers was involved in Stuart's cash-for questions scam.

'All I can say is I'm glad I work for Jon, and not that bastard Stuart Dumass. Poor you,' she said, rubbing my back and decimating a good section of frock. 'Speaking of which, where is Jon? I imagined he'd be picking you up, actually.'

'Oh, no, I told him I'd make my own way here,' I lied. I was able to avoid further enquiry by pointing out my ex. 'There's Emmanuel over there,' I hissed, spotting him snorting up a glass of champagne from a waitress's tray.

Despite my great dream of bringing him to his knees with the sight of me, I felt strangely disinterested in parading my dress – what was left of it. 'What a nerve he's got, showing up here after dumping me.'

'I thought it was mutual?' Alice recollected.

'So it was. Still doesn't mean he has the right to come here, especially when he knows I'm likely to have been invited.'

'Well, he is an art critic, Sass.'

'Whose side are you on?' I asked hotly. A combination of hunger and lack of Jon was conspiring to turn me into a shrew.

Alice ignored me and pulled my hand. 'Let's go check out the work.' She gave my arm a firm tug so as to avoid further discourse. I followed in her slipstream as she shoved her way through the intelligentsia.

It was around about the point that we reached the six-pack of frozen blood that I finally spotted Jon. He was looking v. cool, as always. His hair was slicked back and his tan was shown to its best advantage against the backdrop of the whitewashed walls. He was wearing the Ozwald Boateng tie I'd bought him. The only problem was, he was also wearing a leggy brunette.

But as I froze and took stock of the horror of my predicament, I realised that the worst was yet to come. I had put my fist to my mouth to stop myself crying out when the leggy brunette turned around and I recognised who it was.

I looked at Alice. She looked at me, and said something like, 'I'm so sorry, Saskia.'

I knew in that instant that Alice wasn't in the least bit surprised by the identity of the scarlet woman. She'd known all along.

I watched her as she bit her lower lip and prevaricated over who I wanted to hit most. Jon? Alice? Or his leggy brunette?

Jon spotted me first. And sensing he was thinking about someone other than her, the leggy brunette looked to see what he was focusing on. She and I made direct and deadly eye contact. If looks could kill, she should by rights have fallen dead on the spot.

All around me people were knocking back bubbly, scoffing down canapés and talking loudly and knowledgeably about the latest sensation. Standing there in my ear plugs, staring at my best friend and my lover, the only sensation I felt was betrayal. It was the oldest feeling in the world, but that night Jon and Sophie were giving it a fresh interpretation.

Ways to Deal with Men who Let you Down (New Immorality Initiative)

1 Remember, puerile behaviour does help. It really does. Collect all clothing he has left at your flat and all underwear and place in bleach, then dry and iron, singeing where poss. Post the remains to him.

2 Keep anything that suits you, natch.

3 Attend public events in his clothing – parade your new kit proudly.

4 Sneak into his flat while he is on holiday and sow his carpet with lawn seed, stick the heating on full. If poss, activate the sprinkler system, otherwise water liberally.

5 Imply to mutual female friends that he may have given you herpes.

6 Imply to mutual female friends that you may have given him herpes.

7 Get a new boyfriend richer than him. Forget better-looking – his wallet and his balls are the only places you can really hurt a man.

8 Tell him you're over him and admit to faking orgasms. Who are you kidding? You did fake orgasms.

9 If all the above fails to raise your spirits, sob yourself to sleep. Time is the best healer. Sounds pathetic but it's true.

I ended up at Albert's flat in Bayswater around nine o'clock, by which time there was virtually nothing left of my dress and even less of my self-esteem. I was sobbing and ranting incoherently, and as if to match my mood, it had started to rain. The cab driver closed the adjoining partition, which sort of summed up what I wanted to do with that evening.

'I've been betrayed,' I wailed, running straight into Sal's chest as he opened the door.

It took a while for me to register that they had visitors, a couple of older men with suave accents and designer clothes. They had probably been enjoying an urbane evening, chatting, drinking and listening to music like civilised adults – that is, they were before I charged banshee-like into their midst.

I wasn't taking in the details that night, though – they could have been having group sex and I wouldn't have noticed. Albert was slumped on his bean bag nursing a cup of tea, and I threw myself on him like a cocker spaniel.

'Albert, I've been betrayed!' I snotted into his neck. He smelt of hair product, cologne and maleness which made me feel even more tragic.

An old Aqua single was playing – 'I'm a Barbie girl, in a Barbie world, it's fantastic – I'm made of plastic!'

I wished more than anything that I was made of plastic. Thinking about this made me sob all the harder.

Albert craned his neck and said something to his guests

that I didn't quite catch because I was howling so hard, but a few moments later I heard the door close. Albert let me cry, patting me on the back and saying there, there type things. He kept making soothing noises while he rummaged for, and lit, two cigarettes. One for him and one for me, but when I tried to smoke it, I inhaled so hard half the filter flew up my throat.

I was glad he didn't ask me to explain. I couldn't have strung a coherent thought together, let alone sentence. The image of Jon wrapped around my best friend made my breaths come in loud, congested gulps.

Sal sat on the other side of Albert facing me and pulled funny faces, but nothing helped. All I could think of was how I'd been betrayed by my best friend and my lover, and how I was going to be turning thirty in a few days' time and how my life was total rubbish.

Albert sent Sal off to get me a cup of tea, then he held me by my shoulders and looked into my swollen, bloodshot eyes.

'Saskia?' he asked solemnly. 'Do you want me to slap you?' Which shows what a gentleman he was; most men in my experience wouldn't have bothered to ask.

Suddenly coming to my senses and remembering my cheek capillaries, I decided I didn't want a slap and managed to get out her name. 'Sophie,' I gurgled through the tears and the snot. 'Sophie, with Jon.'

You can probably imagine how mortified I was, when, instead of charging off to get a weapon or saying something suitably hateful about her, Albert laughed.

'Sorry, darling!' he screamed through his howls of mirth. 'But judging by the way you look, I thought, well we all thought.' He collapsed in a pool of giggles. Sal came over and gave me a big squeeze.

His laughter brought me round a hell of a lot faster than a slap ever could. 'How can you laugh like that? Can't you see, I'm devastated, I've been violated.'

'Well, yes, you have, but not in the way we thought,' Albert explained between guffaws. 'I'm laughing with relief. We thought you must have been raped. You were in such a state. I mean, your dress. Where is your dress, by the way?'

'What?' I asked, feeling v. confused and a bit deaf with it.

'Your dress! Where is it,' he shouted. 'And what the hell are those yellow things protruding from your ears?'

I put my hands to my ears and pulled out the ear plugs. Albert grimaced as if I'd just picked my nose. 'I put them in because the opening was so loud. Anyway, what about my dress?' I insisted, feeling a bit hot under the collar now. I mean, here I was, seeking succour from my friend and confidant only to be ridiculed, derided and mocked about my state of dress and a pair of ear plugs.

'Well, where is it?' he asked.

That was when I looked down and saw what a mess the dress was. Thank goodness I was wearing my best Agent Provocateur underwear.

Little by little, tea by tea, I told them the whole sorry story. Starting from the first time Alice told me that Jon fancied me, followed by the time I first snogged him, to how I felt now that I'd seen him snogging Sophie.

'I blame Sophie the most,' I blubbered into Albert's neck. 'I mean, she's always throwing herself at men.'

Albert held my face in his hands. 'Precisely!' he said. 'So what's the big deal? She's all over Sal every time she sees him. You don't see me howling myself into a state of premature crow's feet, do you?'

'It's true,' Sal agreed as he poured the tea. 'She's carnivorous, that Sophie is. She squeezes my bum when I blow-dry her hair and nibbles my ear when I kiss her goodbye.'

'See, doesn't mean that Sal dives into bed with her. Jon's his own man. Anyone who's ever met that girl knows the score. There *is* such a thing as free will, Saskia my dear.'

I accepted my tea and took a tentative sip. It was hot and sweet. I sort of had to concede that Sal was right. Sophie couldn't be held responsible for her actions. For one, I doubt she even knew I liked Jon. I hadn't exactly confided in her about him. I'd been far too busy dishing on Stuart.

We talked for what seemed like hours about love and friendship, and eventually it dawned on me, with a little help from Albert, that perhaps my feelings for Jon were tied up more with my feelings about turning thirty. Maybe what I was feeling was panic, as opposed to good, clean love.

Sal pointed out that I'd know Jon for years; we'd had plenty of opportunity to get it together. 'So why didn't either of you show much incentive?' he asked.

I told him that all good love stories take that very scenario as their theme. Girl looks for love, only to find it was under her nose all the time.

Sal shook his head. 'Get a life,' he told me. 'You're not as brain-dead as you look, Saskia. If you'd really been stuck on Jon you would have known it and done something about it a long time ago.'

Albert agreed. 'You had every opportunity to join him when he walked out of A SPACE to start Tashco. So why didn't you?'

'Because I was too loyal!'

'You're a proponent of the new immorality, Saskia. A go-after-what-you-want, new-millennium woman.'

I began to giggle. 'This tea is great,' I told them.

They looked at one another and winked. 'That's because it's half vodka,' they admitted.

'I'll tell you why you never did anything about your feelings for Jon before,' Albert confided, waving his cigarette at me. 'Because you were in your twenties, and when you're in your twenties commitment is a dirty word.'

'Oh yeah, and what about Sal? How old are you, Sal?' I asked.

'I don't count. I'm a man who has known his own mind since the cradle.' With that he started snogging Albert, so I didn't really have the opportunity to argue.

When Sophie turned up at Albert's at around eleven, full of apologies, I had totally forgiven her. I'd more or less drunk enough tea to forgive anyone, basically. I told her that there was nothing to be sorry for and that nothing was her fault. I told her that Jon could snog who he wanted because he meant nothing to me and never had.

She sort of looked at me like I might be concealing a deadly weapon up my sleeve. 'I've been looking all over town for you,' she panted.

'Well I think we should be insulted by that, don't you, Sal?' Albert asked his lover.

'Definitely,' agreed Sal as he passed her a cup of tea. 'I would have thought we would be your first port of call.'

Sophie sipped her tea. 'You've got to believe me, Sass, I didn't know you were seeing him. In fact he always told me not to mention anything about us to you. I thought it was because you were so furious about what he did to Stuart. I didn't realise that you *fancied* him. I wouldn't have had anything to do with him if I'd known that.'

We all rolled our eyes. 'Well excuse us if we don't buy that, darling,' Albert scolded.

'What?' she asked, all innocently.

'Nothing,' I told her. 'Go on.'

'That's it, really. He said that you'd always had this huge crush on him and that if we told you about us it would destroy you. I feel so awful now. What a bastard.'

I felt suddenly angry, and some of that no doubt came through in the way I asked Sophie how long she'd been seeing Jon. Albert and Sal discreetly left the room to make some more tea.

'A few months. I mean, I think it was more serious on his part than mine.'

'But he hates you,' I said, remembering the way his eyes always glazed over when Sophie's name was mentioned.

She laughed as she lit a cigarette. 'Is that what he told you? He was obsessed, the man was pathetic. He used to ring me night and day. To tell you the truth, I never liked him that much. Let's face it, he's a pretentious git, but the body! The body makes up for a lot. At the end, though, even that wasn't enough.'

At the thought of the sex I'd enjoyed in his loft I giggled. It felt strangely good dishing on the man who'd let me down with the girl who helped him do it. Or maybe it was just the tea. 'Don't tell me he became a sympathy fuck?'

Sophie gave me a cuddle. 'I thought you were going to kill me. Anyway, I'm glad they've arrested him. I told Stuart he should have done it ages ago, and I meant it.'

'You said *what*?' I asked, completely lost now. 'Who was arrested?'

'Oh, you don't know, do you? After you left, the police arrested Jon. They've been trying to get Stuart to help them with their investigations for months, apparently, but he had some misguided sense of loyalty to the bastard. Only he didn't let on. Turns out he knew Jon was a crook all along.'

'No, you've got it wrong. Surely Stuart's the one they arrested? I mean, the police were looking for *him*.'

Albert and Sal walked in with a fresh pot of tea. 'Stuart's been arrested?' Albert squealed. 'I knew it, I was telling Lady Marshmont this morning.'

I gave him a hard stare.

Sophie took a cup from Sal. 'No, it was the other way around. It was Jon who was using the sale of paintings at auction as a money-laundering scam. See, sleazy businessmen who want questions tabled in Parliament pay Ministers for their complicity. Only, so as to cover up the scam, they get the Minister to buy a painting and then put the painting in at auction.'

'Sure,' I said. 'But there's actually no crime in that. Shrewd investing isn't illegal, even under a Labour government.'

'Yeah, right, but you haven't heard the whole scam. Surprise, surprise, the painting sells for ten times more than the Minister paid for it, the Minister has his bribe and no one's the wiser.'

'Still no crime,' I pointed out.

'It is if the Minister is brought down and the police decide to make a case for conspiracy. Jon could be looking at anything from three to six years.'

A slurp of tea went down the wrong way and I started to choke. 'Jail?' I spluttered, a bit like my aunt does when the nurses at the home try to wrestle her Brillo pads off her.

'Conspiracy can carry a heavy sentence, and that was only part of it. Jon had his fingers in all sorts of dodgy pies. I never did buy that dead aunt story.'

I agreed. 'It sounds like an exhibit, doesn't it? "Dead Aunt" by Jon Tashco.'

'Exactly, and that was why Stuart got rid of him, only he was too decent to let on to you and spoil your image of Jon as Mister Good Guy. He knew you looked up to Jon.'

I blushed.

'So what happened then?' Albert pressed.

'OK, get this, the scam's uncovered and the Minister is investigated. They come looking for Stuart, apparently trying to make a case for conspiracy.'

'Conspiracy?'

'Yeah, Parliament is determined to put a stop to the whole cash-for-questions issue and they wanted to make an example of this guy. And as part of making an example of him, they wanted to pin conspiracy charges on the people involved with the whole scam.'

'My God, I thought they were looking for Stuart?'

'They were, but once they started sniffing around they realised that the problem lay with Jon. Stuart wouldn't give them the full story at first. Out of a misguided sense of loyalty he held back on giving them the information they needed. In the meantime, Jon broke into A SPACE and stole the incriminating records in an effort to hide his crime, and landed himself in an even bigger mess.'

'How much bigger?' Sal asked, completely wrapped up in the story now.

'Apparently, as well as creaming off his commission, he was fiddling his taxes and engaging in a bit of fraud to boot. Over the years he'd become more confident and more corrupt. Seriously, he's in big trouble.'

'And to think Stuart held back on giving the police the dirt. That's so typical of him,' I mused.

'Well, you've changed your tune, darling,' Albert remarked. 'You were having him done for money-laundering a few days ago.'

'Actually,' Sophie continued, 'it was because of Saskia that Stuart eventually had the balls to give the police what they needed.'

'How so?' I asked, thrilled to think I'd been useful in some way.

'The only reason he came clean was because he found that list of yours.'

'What list?' I asked, completely confused now.

'The list of things you hate most about him – the abridged version, apparently.'

I slumped on the sofa. 'Oh, my God, he found my list of the things I hate most about him?'

'The abridged version!' Albert laughed. 'Honestly Sass, your lists will get you into big trouble one day,' he scolded.

Utterly Glamorous Moments to Savour

1   Buying a whole new outfit just for one evening.
2   Going to a party or opening and staggering others with my witty repartee.
3   Wearing frighteningly high shoes by Jimmy Choo or other footwear icon, so that I can see over everyone else's head.
4   Being invited at said party to judge the Turner Prize or other prestigious art event.
5   Having a man so spellbound by my beauty that he falls on his knees in front of all my exes and friends, especially the thinner, more attractive ones.

Utterly Embarrassing Moments to Forget

1   Buying a dress for one night, only to have it dissolve embarrassingly.
2   Going to a party or opening and shocking people with my ear plugs.
3   Wearing frighteningly old shoes and having the heel break.
4   Seeing lover at said party snogging best friend.
5   Having a man so spellbound by my friend's beauty that he falls to his knees in front of fatter friend, ie me.

I got the rest of the story from Alice when I finally arrived home that night. Piers was with her, lounging on the sofa like he was an old friend over to watch the football.

They were listening to a Charlie Parker record and giggled like teenagers sprung by parents when I walked in at around midnight. I don't know what I was expecting, but I sure was shocked at the tableau of domestic felicity I found.

When they saw me they both went into super-supportive-friend mode, only Alice had had more experience in the role and so was the first to fold me in a big cuddle. Piers kept his place on the sofa. I noticed his shoes, placed neatly on the floor beside him. His legs were stretched out comfortably, one foot crossed cosily over the other. Alice was making him feel completely at home.

It was stupid to feel jealous but I did.

'There, there, he was a bastard,' she soothed, clearly thinking she was going to have to mop up tears until breakfast.

I pulled away and smiled bravely, then I reminded her that she had said the same about Emmanuel.

Piers looked up at me and grinned and said something banal like, 'We were wondering when you'd show.' It was a lovely smile but I was too busy clocking the evidence of their evening together.

Two bottles of champagne, Bollinger no less, were on the

coffee table, one of them empty and the other getting that way. I thought of my brief moment in Piers's affections when I had worn the Bolly Boy poncho. It seemed so far away now. How had I ever been roped into fancying Jon? The whole drama was a three-0 aberration of immense proportions: that was the only reasonable excuse I could come up with.

Piers and Alice seemed to be getting on like a house on fire and I felt a bit left out. My initial sense of excitement at running home to tell my flatmate my news had soured.

I mean, it was inevitable that two great people like Alice and Piers should get together. Course they would. After all, they were both American and gorgeous, and hadn't I stood Piers up on our first date? It served me right. Just the same, it was hard not to feel a twinge of the what-might-have-beens.

They told me about how Jon had been cuffed in the middle of the gallery and how the paparazzi had got a million shots. People were hailing it the coolest art event ever. Alice was talking at a mile a minute while Piers stretched out, totally composed, as if he watched people getting nicked every day.

'I mean, some people even thought his arrest was one of the exhibits, sort of like a performance piece.'

'Sounds amazing,' I said, with far more enthusiasm than I felt as I sat down opposite Piers. He lifted the bottle of Bolly to offer me a drink. I declined, explaining that I'd been drinking tea all night (while simultaneously pretending not to ogle him).

He was looking even a billion times better than I remembered, which was already a billion times better than anyone else I'd fancied had looked. Jon seemed positively old and shabby compared to Piers. Keep focusing on *Experiences in White*, I told myself. You can't possibly be even mildly attracted to a man who loved that work enough to buy the whole show. Can you? Er, well . . .

'It will be front page for sure,' Alice announced, looking coyly at Piers. 'I guess I should be feeling horrible, though. This fiasco means I'm out of a job.' She giggled some more.

I looked at her with envy. Oh, to be twentysomething and giggly again! I couldn't think of anything remotely worth giggling about at that moment. Alice and Piers just looked so darn good together. Tearful, that was how I felt.

She was more than a little tipsy, but in her sophisticated, simple black dress and her immaculate, tangle-free hair pulled back into a chignon, she looked like Audrey Hepburn. Bitch. I looked like Jane Russell after a bad peroxide job and a clash with a pair of clippers.

'I don't think you need worry about that,' Piers interrupted, refilling her glass. 'I'll need someone to curate my collection here in London. I'm meeting the architects tomorrow to discuss the plans for a gallery in which to house it.'

'You're kidding!' I exclaimed. 'You're opening a gallery?'

'Something along the lines of the Saatchi gallery, yes. After all, I'll need to store the collection somewhere. Why shouldn't the general public get to see them?'

'Why not indeed?' Alice squealed, giving him a big hug. 'What a great idea!'

I looked on, sick with jealousy, until eventually the bitch within me rose up and said, 'You're going to show *Experiences in White* to the general public?' I didn't actually say the words 'you're mad', but they hung about my remark like the smoggy cloud over London.

'Well, yes, among other things,' he admitted, looking slightly embarrassed. 'Of course, not all the collection will go on show at one time.'

'But this is brilliant!' Alice cried before I could discharge another round of bitchy remarks into the conversation. She looked adorable and utterly cool in her little black dress from Gucci. I looked at what was left of my own vintage remnant. No more than a rag, it barely concealed my admittedly sexy underwear. I looked like Cinderella after the Fairy Godmother's magic had run out.

Alice was positively kittenish with delight. 'I can't believe you're offering me a chance to curate your collection. This is just the greatest.'

Piers looked like a father who'd just given his daughter a Porsche for her birthday. He patted her hand affectionately. I looked just like I felt – consumed with envy.

I steered the conversation back to Jon's arrest and asked a few more questions, but Alice was overexcited and finished off a lot of Piers's sentences for him which I found v. exasperating. Eventually I stood up and said I was going to bed. They waved me off, seemingly happy to see the last of me.

I left them whispering in the living room and closed the door of my room, where I lay awake for most of the night making a mental list of all the biggest mistakes I had made in my life. The chief of which was blowing out Piers that night for Jon, natch.

Rules a Girl should Adhere to after Turning Thirty

1 No is never an answer, just a notion.
2 Size *does* matter.
3 Never eat anything bigger than your head.
4 How to say sorry.
5 How to make champagne cocktails (soak sugar cubes in brandy, add a splash of Cointreau and lashings of champagne).
6 Shun overhead lighting.
7 All men aren't bastards – just some of them.
8 Wish lists do come true.
9 However old I am, I'll never be this young again!

Sophie and I woke up in Claridge's around ten. We'd agreed to spoil ourselves on our last night as twentysomethings. Instead of partying and using men for sex, we elected to spend the night doing face packs, watching *Breakfast at Tiffany's* and toasting our past with mineral water – we had to think of our complexions now.

We'd also compiled a list of men we wanted to sleep with by the time we were forty. I only had two people on my list, and one of them was Jean-Michel Basquiat who was already dead, but I thought just having the one name on the list looked too tragic. Sophie had filled in every sheet of complimentary notepaper in the room with her projected love life, natch.

We unwrapped the presents from our parents over a delicious breakfast of muffins, coffee and champagne cocktails which we made ourselves, using the contents of the minibar and some sugar cubes off the breakfast tray. Sophie said it was a skill every thirtysomething girl should possess.

'Do you feel different, then?' I asked as we gorged.

She crinkled up her nose. 'Sort of, I'm not sure. It might just be the champagne cocktails; I've never drunk them in the morning. Do you suppose we'll have to do this all the time now that we're thirty?'

'Definitely,' I said with my new-found confidence. 'Do you think we'll be all self-assured and mature and not bothered about cellulite and other really *down* stuff? You know, like Alice?'

'Nah. She's American so that doesn't count. She was born with a psychological silver spoon in her mouth. We English girls have to save up.'

The breakfast had been delivered to our room around ten. Unbeknown to the guy who wheeled it in, he was number seven on Sophie's list of men she wanted to sleep with by age forty. It was all I could do to stop her dragging him under the covers there and then. As it was, she gave him a twenty-quid tip.

My mother had given me a book on Monet and five hundred pounds, with a note that I could do worse than put the money into my pension fund. Sophie received a voucher for Cliveden from her father and a pair of Chanel earrings from her mother.

I wondered briefly how my father was and whether he'd found a new woman to buy his socks in Nepal.

'They probably have very nice socks in Nepal,' Sophie mused, dunking a chocolate muffin in her cocktail. 'Maybe he's progressed and become a new man, and he's buying his own socks now.'

We looked at one another and burst out laughing.

It was amazing the way both of us sleeping with Jon had brought us even closer together. Since that night at Albert's, we hadn't stopped sharing sex-with-Jon stories in which Jon always came off the worse for the telling.

'What was it about him that made us fall so hard?' I asked Sophie.

'Humour,' she said. 'Although you know what? I don't think I remember him telling me a single joke.'

'It was the way his eyes crinkled up at the corners – he always looked like he might be about to. I suppose his eyes might droop inside, you know, get that prison droop?'

Sophie shook her head and sipped her cocktail. 'Nah.

They'll send him to one of those farm prisons, those low-security, telly-in-your-room jails.'

'Do you think so?'

'Definitely. He'll probably do a course in white-collar crime or something. I doubt he'll even be compromised in the shower, you know, reaching for the soap.'

I giggled. 'He compromised *me* in the shower.'

Sophie squealed. 'Me too!'

'I had a really loud, expressive orgasm,' I remembered. I treated Sophie to a re-enactment and, like the sport she is, she joined in on the climax.

'So did I!' she said as she panted at the end of the bed. Orgasms can be v. exhausting. 'Fake?' she asked.

'Natch!' I said, and we toasted all the fakes we'd had. Sometimes a fake one can be even more fun than a real one, we decided. That's what boys will never understand.

We made another batch of cocktails and fell about laughing some more. 'I found he came quicker if I made a lot of noise and thrashed about, actually,' I explained reminiscently.

'Exactly. He did go on a bit sometimes, all that thrusting and pumping. I thought he was going to get a puncture. Still, he had nice eyes.'

We toasted Jon's eyes. 'Do you think we can train ours to do that?' I asked her, using my fingers to get the effect.

'Yeah, but it's called crow's feet on girls.'

We'd more or less decided to take a vow of chastity, notwithstanding the men we most wanted to sleep with by forty, natch. They didn't count.

We spent the day at the Aveda beauty salon luxuriating the day away until by seven we were looking utterly gorgeous. Even if we said so ourselves.

Alice had arranged a party for us at Piers's house in Notting Hill. They had been spending a lot of time together, and, being a girl on the edge of thirty, I'd tried to be really mature about it and gave them a wide berth. 'You are turning thirty any day now,' I told myself when I bumped into the two of them hunched furtively over papers. 'Your heart should be gladdened by the sight of young love.' As if.

Alice said they needed to discuss a lot of stuff regarding plans for his collection, but I told her I was turning thirty, not three. I knew the look of true love when I saw it, and Piers's face was etched with it.

Notwithstanding romance, my life was looking up. Even my career was on track. Stuart and I had enjoyed a perfect lunch together the day before. He'd been in Cornwall for a few days, where he was starting up another gallery.

Watching him as he struggled with his bits of rocket salad, I couldn't stop thinking about my list of things I hate about my boss – the Abridged Version, and wondering how he could sit down to lunch with me after all the horrible things I'd written.

God, I was cruel. How could I have hated this good, decent man sitting before me now? Actually, it was easy – even now that he had been exonerated on so many counts, his anal demeanour really got to me. He actually cut up the olives in his salad. It was all I could do not to dive into his bowl and shove the things into his mouth. I managed to restrain myself, natch.

But then I began to worry as he spoke about the new gallery. What if he was moving all the way to Cornwall to get away from me? What if it *was* all my fault, or rather the fault of the list? I decided I had to say something to put the record straight.

I toyed with the idea of blaming my dyslexia but given my track record with that excuse, I didn't hold out much hope. I could always say I'd written the list about another boss, or even blame Sophie by saying that she'd written the list.

Stirring the chocolate powder into the froth of my cappuccino, I knew it would be pointless to ask for a reference, given all the stuff I'd put in that list. Even the new immorality dictated that I had to say *something*.

'Stuart, I just want to say, um.'

'What?'

'Um, I just want to say, um.'

He looked at me curiously, and, noticing that he was wearing chinos and a tweedy jacket, I made a quip about him already looking quite the country gent.

'I'm sick of London,' he sighed heavily as he added sugar to his coffee. 'I can't wait to be shot of the place.' Then he told me how he'd thought of moving to St Ives when the Tate first set up there, but that other matters had kept him in London. I guessed he was referring to Jon.

I nodded sympathetically. 'Do you know what you'll do about A SPACE? I mean, will you close it down immediately or sort of wind it up over a few months? Subtext here, should I sign on now or later?'

'God, no. I wouldn't dream of closing it down. I was rather hoping you would agree to manage it for me. To be honest, I was hoping for a partnership, that is, if you're amenable. There wouldn't be any financial costs; I'd pay you as I do now, of course, although there would be extra remuneration for the added responsibility.'

Responsibility? Remuneration? These words were music to my ears. I practically killed him with kisses, especially when he explained that he'd be employing a financial adviser to handle the boring stuff like loo rolls, leaving me free to curate the shows, liaise with artists and pour Chardonnay.

I had the best boss a girl could ask for. Perhaps I would write a new list and call it Things I Love about My Boss. Point 1: He lives and works at the other end of the country. Yes, that would be a good start.

As part of his new spirit of generosity, Stuart picked up Sophie and me from Claridge's with our bags and drove us to the party. We were both wearing our best frocks. Only Sophie's was a designer label, and mine was a really tight fifties *La Dolce Vita* black dress I'd discovered on a five-pound table at Portobello.

Sophie sat up front with Stuart, and I swear she flirted so hard it's a wonder we didn't crash. I sat in the back wondering what I was going to say to Piers when I saw him. Perhaps I would act all grande dame-ish and swoop into his room like Gertrude Whitney Vanderbilt. Or maybe I would do a mysterious Latin number, like Georgia O'Keeffe.

On the steps of Piers's house in Notting Hill, Sophie pulled me aside and asked me in a whisper if I thought she had a chance with Stuart and would I mind her sleeping with my boss. I felt like the Pope giving my blessing to their union. Maybe that was what being a spinster at thirty was all about. Sitting on the sidelines of romance, watching other people get the touchdowns.

Everyone screamed 'Surprise!' when we walked in, which sort of surprised us given that we knew we were coming to our own party. Then they fell on us like teeny-boppers on a boy band, burying us in a pile of presents and kisses. The champagne flowed, the good cheer fizzed and I watched with envy as Sophie and Stuart snuggled up on the sofa and started their foreplay. 'Disgusting,' I thought to myself.

'Hiya,' Alice said, appearing sheepishly from the kitchen. I'd been avoiding her the last few days, and she'd taken to behaving like she'd actually done something wrong, creeping around and doing lots of tidying up.

'How's it feel being thirty, then?' she asked.

'Pretty much the same as twenty-nine, only now I'm actually contemplating sinking my birthday money into a pension,' I told her as I filled my hand with some canapés from a nearby tray.

She laughed as if it was like the joke of the century, then passed me a thick black envelope.

It looked like it was made of liquorice. I gave it a sniff. 'What's this? Your notice to quit the flat?' I joked.

'How did you know? I mean no, it's not, but I mean, oh God, I wasn't going to tell you.'

'Tell me what?' She was going to tell me that she was moving in with Piers, I knew it. God, talk about quick off the mark – these twentysomethings don't let the grass grow.

'I'm going back to New York. Piers wants me to spend some time with the curator of his collection out there. Thing is, I'll be away for about three months. I'll be back and forth, and I can still pay my share of the flat but . . . ? Are you mad?'

I didn't want to say. 'So what's this?' I asked, holding up the envelope.

'Your present. I thought black was appropriate.'

I raised an eyebrow.

'Death of the old, new beginnings – oh, just open it.'

I tore my finger along the side of the envelope and pulled out the contents. I held up a British Airways envelope.

Alice squealed. 'First class! We're going first class! Two weeks!' She threw her arms around me. 'Piers paid. I mean, I've got you something else as well, but he paid for the tickets. He thought you might like to go! We leave next week. Isn't it great?'

'Um, yeah, it is. Great.'

She hugged me again. 'I've checked with Stuart, about time off and stuff. It's all fine. Can you believe it? We're going to New York!' She was jumping up and down and talking at a hundred words a second. My head was spinning with all sorts of conflicting concepts. Foremost was Piers. Where was he? I hadn't spotted him.

'That's so great!' I agreed, trying to sound v. enthused.

Well, I was v. enthused. So why wasn't I jumping around all over the place like Alice, a voice inside me said? My mother was right: I aim too high. Even first class wasn't enough for me.

The A-list of Valuable People you should Know by Thirty

1   A hairdresser who can make you look sublime, and sort out all your problems in a blow-dry.
2   Someone you can trust with your secrets.
3   A man who can reach your G-spot just by saying your name.
4   A celebrity who can get you invited to all the fabulous A-list parties.
5   Friends who you know you can never deserve.
6   A good boss – preferably one who lives a long way away.
7   A man who will buy you vintage Givenchy.
8   A lover with taste in art.

I pushed open the door to Piers Dexter's bedroom. OK, so I knew it was trespassing by any other name, but as a girl of the new immorality I was prepared to blur the term. After all, there was a party going on in his flat – he had to expect a little curiosity on the part of his guests.

I was nervous not just of being sprung but of what I might find. Evidence of further tastelessness à la 'White Mood Swing', perhaps? Or blow-up dolls, chintz curtains, a waterbed or Piers, kissing someone else? But thankfully the room was empty of all such devices.

There was light emanating from an open cupboard, part of a discreetly hidden walk-in wardrobe. The curtains were open revealing a view over the communal gardens, and I fought off a sudden vision of Piers and me having a picnic on a rug while chortling children ran cheerfully around the exotic shrubbery. Not that I'd know a shrub exotic or otherwise if I fell over one, but you get the idea.

Looking around me, I saw that it was a simply decorated room, ash flooring, wooden blinds and a big antique four-poster bed – not a waterbed ripple in sight. The art consisted of a Damien Hirst butterfly painting over the bed, and an amusing Dinos and Jake sculpture in the corner that made me smirk. It didn't really go with *Experiences in White*. And, once again, I wondered if Piers was involved in Jon's conspiracy.

I walked over to a wooden stand displaying the most abundant arrangement of white flowers of every description, and swooned at the delicious scent, redolent of the cologne Piers wore. It was all v. tasteful, simple without being clinical. Expensive-looking. In short, not the decor I would associate with a man prepared to throw money at a crappy show like Hewit's. I crept in.

I told myself it wasn't snooping; I was naturally interested in the man who had been indirectly responsible for turning my career around. But I didn't fool myself for a minute, natch.

My interest intensified when I noticed a huge parcel leaning across a wall at the far end of the room. It was taller than me and covered with calico. I decided that I might just sneak over and lift a corner of the cloth for a peek – and that was the point when Piers appeared from the en suite.

He was holding a long, white beaded frock in front of him and when he saw me, he jumped. 'You've sprung me,' he said, and then gave a more or less embarrassed chuckle.

Surely that was my line, but given the frock he was holding against himself, I saw his point.

'I'm so sorry, I had no idea. I mean, not that I judge you or anything – if you want to wear frocks in the comfort of your own home, then by all means go right ahead,' I told him tolerantly.

'No, Saskia. You don't understand.'

I put my hand up to calm him. 'You don't have to explain a thing, I mean, it's very fashionable in some circles, especially among men of a certain age. My brother Martin became a monk and now he wears frocks all the time, only he calls them something Tibetan, I think, but it amounts to the same thing, doesn't it?' I was rambling.

'Saskia, what are you talking about?'

'The dress. I don't want you to think I judge you.'

'The dress. The dress is for you. I mean I hadn't wrapped it because it smelt kind of musty from the shop. I was letting it air. Here, see, it's a vintage Givenchy. Alice said you loved old clothes.'

He held it out.

For once in my life I was speechless. A thousand glass beads twinkled as he turned the lights on. He passed it to me and I gasped. I'd never held anything so beautiful in my hands before. I was stunned. 'Thank you. I mean, this is the best thing I've ever seen in my life. I can't believe it. Can I hug you?'

He didn't wait for an answer. With the dress crushed between us, we clung to one another for what seemed like the whole evening. He smelt like one of my dreams, the one where the most gorgeous man ever takes me into his arms and tells me he's in love with my sister Rebecca. Only Piers had never even met Rebecca, so this was much better.

He broke the embrace first and kissed my forehead. 'When I saw you lift the cloth, I thought you were going to *kill* me.' He smiled at me like small children do in the gallery when I catch them pawing a painting, and I tell them I'm going to report them to the police.

'I don't understand,' I told him, holding the frock against me in case he'd changed his mind.

'You didn't see it, did you?'

'See what?' I asked, completely confused now.

'Well, I'd better come clean anyway. Lift the cloth,' he instructed, then he pointed towards the parcel.

I went over and did as he said.

Experiences in White, the whole show, every painting including 'White Mood Swing' was there, tied together with rope. I turned to him, v. troubled. 'But why? I don't understand. You want them for your *home*? I looked around the classically decorated room and the totally cool artworks already adorning it. 'I thought you'd bought them for your collection.'

'I know. I'm really sorry, but I can't stand the sight of them. I just can't handle them. I've agreed with Stuart that he'll take them back; he's going to show them in St Ives.'

'I see,' I said, not seeing at all. 'So why did you buy them?'

'Because of *you*, you jerk.' It was Alice's voice, and we both spun around. She was looking v. chic as she walked towards us. 'He saw you, fell in love and bought the show as a way of meeting you.'

'What?' I looked from one to the other.

She was grinning. 'Don't you get it, even now? The man's got a serious crush on you. Don't ask me why, I've tried to talk him out of it, but he is awestruck. I think it was the Israeli army boots. Anyway, I don't want to disturb you, but I found this in the passage. Someone must have dropped it.' She passed me what I instantly recognised to be Claridge's notepaper. Piers snatched it and began to read.

I watched him while a pilot light ignited in my stomach, setting all my organs on fire. Piers raised his head and gave me an impenetrable look.

'The thing about lists is that they give you an idea of where you are going,' I told him. 'Just an idea. A direction. Doesn't mean you, er, follow them or anything, course not. The thing is, they act as a more or less subconscious map. That's it – a map,' I explained as if I actually knew what I was talking about.

'They can also get you into such a lot of trouble if they fall into the wrong hands,' Piers remarked.

'Oh, Saskia, you've not been making lists again, have you?' Alice sighed, peering over Piers's shoulder to read the list. 'You know, they can be misinterpreted.'

'Just like art,' Piers laughed.

I can't remember if I replied or if Alice was still there, but whatever was said, I kissed him, long, hard and without asking permission first.